Praise for Cassandra Dean

Cassandra Dean spins a story where this reader could share in the ache, and desire, that embraces the characters and brings out true emotion.
–The Romance Studio

It takes a special kind of talent to craft a compelling [sic] story–it takes very unique talent indeed to create characters as engaging and sympathetic as those found in Cassandra Dean's stories.
–The Romance Reviews

With just a whisper, a caress, or a simple kiss, Ms. Dean takes the reader on an adventure full of hedonistic pleasure as well as bittersweet moments.
– Coffee Time Romance

Silk & Scholar

THE SILK SEREIS BOOK 4

Cassandra Dean

Cassandra acknowledges where she is based are the
traditional lands of the Kaurna people and respects
their spiritual relationship with their Country.

By Cassandra Dean

Enslaved
Teach Me
Scandalous
Rough Diamond
Fool's Gold
Emerald Sea
Silk & Scandal
Silk & Scorn
Silk & Scars
Silk & Scholar
Silk & Scarlet
Slumber
Awaken
Finding Lord Farlisle
Rescuing Lord Roxwaithe
Stealing Lord Stephen
Persuading Lady Penelope

Dedication

To everyone who's ever been made to feel they care 'too much'.
Believe me when I say: There is no too much.

Silk &
Scholar

THE SILK SEREIS BOOK 4

Cassandra
Dean

Prologue

Newspaper clipping sent to Miss Henrietta Wilding-Marsh, received 5 January 1841

3ʳᵈ March, 1841 – Lecture series on the finer points of criminal law, featuring examples from recent cases. Prof. M. N. B. Childers, LL.M; Prof S. V. Marlowe, LL.M; Mr. E. S. Wickham, Esq, Barrister-at-Law; C. A. Hiddleson, LL.B.

No note included

***

No reply

***

Newspaper clipping sent to Miss Henrietta Wilding-Marsh, received 13 April 1841

5ᵗʰ May, 1841 – Lecture series on the Saksian

Tort and its relation to Modern Law. Prof. K. H Trengove; C. A. Hiddleson, LL.B.

***

No reply

***

Newspaper clipping sent to Miss Henrietta Wilding-Marsh, received 5 July 1841

...this author was surprised to find himself impressed with the comments of Lord Christopher Hiddleston, LL.B. While the lecturer is young, his grasp on the nuances of prima facie determination and how, in some instances, to bring about the disproving of such evidence is extraordinary and could be termed groundbreaking. This author believes we will hear more from the young lord in years to come.

***

Wisteria Cottage, Cambridge, 29 August 1841

Sir,
Cease sending these absurd news clippings. Why you should imagine I have any desire for knowledge of your whereabouts or circumstance, I cannot say. Indeed, the finest day of my life was your graduation day, when I knew you would soon be far from Cambridge and I should never have to see you again or endure your woeful and wholly incorrect

arguments on points of law. Therefore, you can imagine my dismay when I opened our mail and discovered you thought it prudent to send news clippings articulating your circumstances, and then to receive another and another... I can assure you, sir, I am not interested.

I must conclude you are simple, if you can infer from the complete lack of response I am in the slightest interested in your career (if indeed it can be termed such). From these clippings, all I see is a man sadly chasing after fame and notoriety, as if either were a worthy goal to achieve.

I reiterate, sir. Cease your correspondence. I have better things to do.

I have the honour to remain,
Your servant,
Miss H. R. Wilding-Marsh

***

Newspaper clipping sent to Miss Henrietta Wilding-Marsh, received 26 January 1842

...of interest is Lord Christopher Hiddleston, who has taken society by storm with his popular lecture series on Strange and Deliciously Scandalous legal cases. Many young ladies seem taken with the handsome Lord Christopher, and this author has heard many a whisper on his fine eyes and shockingly fiery hair, setting young hearts ablaze with passion... for the law.

***

Wisteria Cottage, Cambridge, 27 February 1842

Sir,

I ask, again, that you cease this correspondence. While it is admirable you attempt to keep the newsheets in print, the amount of paper wasted is obscene.

Further, why have you included newsprint which has been defaced with the most turgid and overwrought prose I've had the misfortune to read written over every blank space available? I do not enjoy this Gothic romance craze and am offended you assume I do. I have corrected this offence to English literature and return to you for your edification. Note, in particular, the gaps in logic that beggar belief. It is a Gothic, it is true, but even a Gothic must adhere to common sense.

I have the honour to remain,
Your servant,
Miss H. R. Wilding-Marsh

***

Newspaper clipping sent to Miss Henrietta Wilding-Marsh, received 4 June 1842

...the lecture itself was an irregular affair, with his lordship taking centre stage. Despite his youth, his lordship commanded a degree of knowledge on the subject, even if his views were highly inflammatory and dangerously speculative. This author found himself at times prone to disregard aspects of his lordship's argument, which could be attributed to his youth but also to the sensational nature of his comments.

***

Wisteria Cottage, Cambridge, 4 June 1842

Sir,

I cannot believe you would pervert the law with such vulgar and deliberately sensational lectures. What possesses you, to seek fame and notoriety through such measures?

Oh, but I shouldn't question, should I? After all, it is you and you've always been contrary and prone to bluster. You never admired the law for its purity, for its incontrovertible truth. For you, it is merely a way to twist and dodge, until all that is left is a perversion of the intent. Nothing in your behaviour since Cambridge has changed my mind on this perception. Nothing ever will.

Cease this correspondence. Surely you are spending a fortune in postage?

I have the honour to remain,

Your servant,

Miss H. R. Wilding-Marsh

Postscript, Why do you continue to include these scribbles of prose? I find them beyond tedious. While the word use shows some grasp of the English language, the structure is trite and stale. Again, the author has breached logic, which I realise is an oxymoron for Gothic novels, but in the interests of consistency I have marked these clearly in my response.

***

Newspaper clipping sent to Miss Henrietta Wilding-Marsh, received 15 November 1844

(highlighted section) Graduates: Lord C.A Hiddleston, LL.M.

***

Wisteria Cottage, Cambridge, 27 December 1844

Sir,
Courtesy dictates I congratulate you on your recent graduation. A Master in Law is indeed an achievement. However, I must reiterate, yet again, that you cease this correspondence.
I have the honour to remain,
Your servant,
Miss H. R. Wilding-Marsh

***

Newspaper clippings sent to Miss Henrietta Wilding-Marsh, received 12 March 1845

...it must be noted there were few dry eyes this morning when Lord C— H—, brother of a certain Earl H—, took to ship to voyage across the Channel. This author confesses to a sniffle or two when contemplating the notion we will not enjoy his presence at the balls and gatherings of this season. However, we Britons are a generous people, and we cannot keep such finery to ourselves. It is best Lord C— H— is unleashed upon the world, to bring his gentility and his wit to the Continent and the peoples

contained within.

...a Gothic serial is causing a sensation. Though the Author remains Anonymous, the tale of the ingénue Minerva, the dastardly Orlando and the stalwart Benvuto has captured the imagination of all within Society. Each instalment is consumed eagerly, and the wait for the next is interminable. Will Minerva discover Orlando's perfidy? That is the question on this author's lips.

***

Wisteria Cottage, Cambridge, 27 March 1845

Good God. The drivel they spout about you. I cannot— I fair— it boggles the mind. Truly. My mind is boggled.

I can only assume you don't read my letters, as your articles continue. In fact, I am absolutely certain you won't read this. After all, you're probably swanning about the Continent beleaguering some other poor girl with your pathetic news clippings. And to prove such...Mrs. Appleby called me strange again yesterday. I don't believe she meant to, but she is rather good at saying what she's thinking and, yes, she thinks me strange. I suppose if I were a normal girl, I would want the things other girls do, to be married, to be a mother, and I do want those things, I just want...more. In any case, it doesn't trouble me to be called strange, especially not by Mrs. Appleby.

There. I dare you to comment, sir.
I have the honour to remain,
Your servant,
Miss H. R. Wilding-Marsh

Postscript, There is little point complaining of the inclusion of the blasted Gothic serial article, isn't there?

***

Various Viennese newspaper clippings regarding R v. Blaubart sent to Miss Henrietta Wilding-Marsh, received 19 February 1846
Note: German translation enclosed.

***

Wisteria Cottage, Cambridge, 19 February 1846

I know how to read German.
P.S. My father thanks you for the information.
P.P.S. I did not request this information, no matter what your tiny brain infers from my letters.

***

Newspaper clipping sent to Miss Henrietta Wilding-Marsh, received 27 December 1846

Lord C— H— has returned from abroad and has been revealed to the Author of the Gothic Tales that have taken London by storm! The wily lord penned the adventures of Minerva, Orlando and Benvuto, his publisher Mr. G. R. Mannifred has revealed, with the serial being compiled into a series of volumes available soon for purchase. When pressed, Mr. Mannifred also let slip Lord C— is working on a new novel! Based upon the case of the notorious Baron von Blaubart, his lordship's new tale will embellish the already scandalous details. Readers may remember the Bad Baron was exonerated of the charge of attempted murder of his fourth wife. Readers may further remember the baron has been singularly unfortunate in his choice of wives, with three of them expiring prior to this latest scandal and all three under suspicious circumstances.

This author cannot wait to devour this new novel and can only wonder—What new nefarious tales will his lordship have brought us, inspired by distant shores?

***

Wisteria Cottage, Cambridge, 27 December 1846

Sir,

Luck was on my side as I did not receive this clipping until after Christmas, and thus it was very merry indeed without your intrusive presence, or the knowledge that you are wasting your law degree. You have such privilege and—

To illustrate: I attempted to attend a lecture last week and was turned away. They thought to bar me from the lecture series, though there was no direct instruction that women could not attend. I merely wished to listen to the findings of Mr. Downey and perhaps even congratulate him on his recent court win, but this is something I cannot do. It is such a small thing, insignificant really, and yet it is denied me. And you…you throw your privilege away and—

I cannot believe you would discard your calling

as if it were nothing, however, what else should I expect? You've always shown yourself to be an unfortunate sort of person, but this goes beyond the pale. A Gothic novelist? Really?

No. I cannot talk of this. It makes me too furious.

Though I know you won't adhere to it, I shall state it anyway. Cease this correspondence.

I have the honour to remain,
Your servant,
Miss H. R. Wilding-Marsh

***

Various newspaper clippings dated from 22 March 1846 to 30 August 1847 sent to Miss Henrietta Wilding-Marsh, received 4 September 1847

***

Wisteria Cottage, Cambridge, 5 September 1847

Why have you sent me this too-thick packet of paper containing such utter drivel? Do you wish me to do you a murder? Because I will. I will track you done and do away with you in such a manner so as no one will ever discover your remains.

As I'm sure it has kept you up all night, you'll be no doubt pleased to know I have reconciled myself to your status as a Gothic novelist. I admit you have achieved success with it and appear to be popular with the masses. This determination was in part helped by your lack of communication. Two glorious years of silence. Bliss

And because you do not read this, and I have to tell someone or fair explode: Today I think I disturbed Mr. Hartley. He had a distinctly wild look to his eye as I debated the merits of recent common law judgements. I am used to this look in a man's eye, especially as my father wears it often, but I persevered. How am I to learn anything, if I do not push?

I wonder what London would be like. Maybe I should move in with Gwen. If I had the funds I should do so in a heartbeat. Although she has been acting rather cagey lately. In her last letter, she seemed distracted, and she mentioned one of the chambers clients twice. Specifically twice. *The Duke of Sowrith. I shall have to ask her in my next letter why she made mention of him. Twice.*

******

Newspaper clipping sent to Miss Henrietta Wilding-Marsh, received 9 November 1847

All of London is abuzz with news the latest Gothic novel from Lord C— H— will arrive in a matter of days! What salaciousness will this next story hold?

The man himself set hearts aflutter across London when he was seen on the promenade of Hyde Park, looking delectable in garb designed by 'The Tailor' himself, M. Brodeur. As our readers know, M. Brodeur is the most respected men's clothier in the city, such he has earned the simple moniker "The Tailor" as no one comes near his skill.

This author has secured a ticket to his lordship's reading of his latest Work, but if you cannot say the same, it is too late. The reading is sold out.

Lord C— H— will speak in the Receiving Room of Wiltshirton House, from Tuesday until Saturday next.

***

Wisteria Cottage, Cambridge, 15 November 1847

...Gwen is to marry, and not just marry, but to brilliantly marry. The Duke of Sowrith. I cannot fair believe it. I had no idea she had formed an attachment to him, but she tells me she had written him for over a year and slowly built a friendship. Then, she was summoned to his estate, and they fell in love.

I don't quite know how I feel about this. On the one hand, I am so, so happy for her. She is practically incandescent with joy. But, on the other, I am losing my friend. She will reside in Dartmoor. Dartmoor. Even further away.

But she is happy, and I cannot complain. I cannot.

Again, though I know it makes no difference and you don't read these letters, I must, at the very least try.

Cease. Cease with your stupid articles, your smug accomplishments.

I. Do not. Care.

***

Newspaper clipping sent to Miss Henrietta Wilding-Marsh, received 3 April 1849

...a certain Lord who writes novels of the Gothic persuasion was spotted shopping for new luggage today. Could it be his lordship intends another voyage?

***

Wisteria Cottage, Cambridge, 3 April 1849

Almost two years without word from you. I started to believe myself one of the blessed.

I can only hope you have chosen to travel abroad. Perhaps you will again disremember my address and leave me in peace for years, although I do not know what is worse: knowing the articles will arrive with some regularity; or waiting for them for months on end only to be lulled into a false sense of security when one, inevitably, arrives.

However, I count myself fortunate that I do not have to deal with you in person. In all these years, it has been correspondence only and that can be ignored.

...Why don't I ignore it?

In any event, I wish you well on your journey and hope you will find whichever country you visit so agreeable you will stay.

I have the honour to remain,
Your servant,
Miss H. R. Wilding-Marsh

Chapter One

HEELS JITTERING AGAINST WORN carpet, Etta kept her gaze trained on the drawing room door. Not ten minutes had passed since her arrival at Bennett Close, and she'd spent all of them in this room, staring at the door as impatience ran her ragged. The ridiculously jovial butler who'd shown her to the room had announced the Duchess of Sowrith only just arrived after her long journey from Dartmoor, and while it was highly unorthodox to receive visitors so soon, he was certain the duchess would attend to her once she saw fit to do so. Etta had scowled at the man's pomp but hadn't enlightened him as to her relationship with the duchess. She'd discovered, after he'd departed, pacing the length of the room did little to soothe her, and so she'd seated herself on this chaise, arms folded over her stomach and gaze locked to the door.

Exhaling, she forced herself to think on other

things. Bennett Close had been shuttered for as long as she could remember, a grim townhouse she and Gwen had often contrived to walk past, morbidly fascinated by the imposing blight on the otherwise pristine townhouses lining Lensfield Road. Though now occupied, the admittedly grand house had the look of the long neglected, the façade bearing faint marks of the ivy that had once climbed the stonework. Even this drawing room displayed signs of neglect, subtle though they were. The carpets were a little too worn, the drapes beaten but old and faded. Freshly cut flowers gave the room a cheery brilliance, but even the hasty cleaning and a spot of colour couldn't disguise the occupancy was of a recent design.

Fingers digging into her forearms, she turned her contemplation from the room and instead willed the door to open. Because when it did, she would finally see Gwen. Gwen, her dearest and closest friend. Gwen, who'd relocated to London in pursuit of employment when it became apparent her father's ailing health would no longer allow him to provide for the Parkes family. Gwen, who she'd not seen in an age, and even then, it had been almost in passing and all too brief.

Gwen, who was now the Duchess of Sowrith and consequently lived even farther away at the ducal estate in Dartmoor.

The door to the drawing room opened silently, such that if she hadn't been watching it so intently, she wouldn't have noticed. The jovial butler stepped into the room, his beaming visage seeming to suggest he was overjoyed to be delivering his announcement. "Her Grace, the Duchess of—"

Joy flooded her. Launching to her feet, she threw herself at Gwen, flinging her arms about her.

"You are back!"

Her friend stumbled under the onslaught but steadied herself to return the hug just as fierce. "I know! I've so missed you."

"Not as much as I missed you." Pulling back, she couldn't stop grinning. "Did you travel well?"

"As well as can be expected." Leading Etta to the chaise, Gwen sat, arranging her travelling coat of soft green wool about her. "How did you know we had arrived?"

"I have my sources." She eyed Gwen's travel wear. "That coat is hideously expensive, isn't it? No point even asking where you found it."

A blush reddened her friend's cheeks. "It's not that expensive."

"I'd wager it was more than what I spent on my entire wardrobe in the last year."

Her blush deepened. "Be quiet," she said, punching Etta in the shoulder.

"Ow," Etta said mildly.

"And what do you mean you have your sources?"

Rubbing her shoulder, she asked, "Pardon?"

"You said you had your sources, knowing when we'd arrived. Who were they?"

She opened her mouth to answer, but Gwen held up her hand. "Actually, don't tell me. I want to be able to plead ignorance to the authorities when they come to take you away."

"Oh, please," she said. "As if you wouldn't be by my side, holding the shovel as we mire ourselves further."

"True," Gwen mused. "Too true."

Her smile was beginning to hurt her face, but she couldn't seem to stop. She had so missed Gwen.

Arranging her hands in her lap, Gwen raised her brows expectantly. "Tell me everything."

Everything? Oh lord, where to start... "There is nothing to tell. My studies continue. Planning on the school is frustrating." She brightened. "The sculls are scheduled for Wednesday. You are attending, aren't you?"

"Of course. I wouldn't miss the sculls if I could possibly help it. Cambridge is going to annihilate Oxford."

"As if it were ever in doubt."

"Agreed. How is your father?"

She blinked. That was a sudden change of subject. Her father? "He is well."

"He is well?"

"Yes." Confusion drew her brows. Gwen never asked after her father. She knew there was little point. "Have you a particular question?"

"No. No, I was—" Smiling, Gwen shook her head. "It is of no matter. You are here, and we should be discussing better things than your father. How goes the scholarship fund?"

"It's there."

A frown creased her friend's brow. "We need that fund. We have the means to build the school, but if we don't have scholarships, we won't have an inaugural class."

"I know this."

"It's only this is vitally important."

"I know that, too." Honestly, she knew how important the scholarship fund was. Years and years ago, she had posited there should be a law school for women. She and Gwen could not be the only women in existence who wished to make the law their passion, and eventually their profession. They would talk endlessly of their school, the courses they would run, the heights their graduates would reach. When Gwen had married the duke, she suddenly had the means to make it happen. And so, she had.

A flurry of letters had traversed the roads between Cambridge and Sowrithil as they worked through a plan. Gwen had warned it would be nigh on impossible. She had explicitly stated the problems inherent in such a venture, not to mention the opposition they would garner from nigh on everyone. The warnings had only made Etta more determined to bring the school into effect. She'd sent a thirteen-page letter stating all the arguments for a school and a general thumbing of her nose at those who sought to oppose them.

Gwen's response had been one line only: When shall we start?

So for over a year, they had been working on plans. Gwen had wanted to call it a finishing school to placate the masses, but Etta had held out for a college. The Sowrith Law College for Women was mere months for completion and the subsequent opening…provided they had students. Hence, the scholarship fund.

Her greatest wish was to make it so any woman who desired it could argue law, in court and in lectures, and not resort as she had to ambushing law students in the local pub. Especially not when there were students who were argumentative for the sake of it, taking the opposing view no matter how outrageous and laughing at her with wicked dark eyes.

She scowled. Lord, what made her think of him?

Gwen rubbed her forehead. "Maybe it is as well

we are holding these events. It will bring some notoriety to the school. We should be able to gather some support and shore up the support we already have. I have the schedule."

"Oh, good. I was thinking on it and I thought we should have an afternoon tea with the three speakers where patrons can pay a 'donation' to attend and have access to them."

Gwen stared at her. "And this is to be organised how?"

She waved her hand. "We can make it happen. I've already secured the agreement of two of the speakers."

"I don't have time—"

"I know you don't. I will take care of it."

"This isn't going to be like the time you organised that bake sale, is it?"

She felt her cheeks heat. "Of course not." And had it really been her fault the labels for salt and sugar were so similar in the Parkes' kitchen?

"Two of the speakers?"

"Yes."

"The third has not agreed?"

"The third could not agree, as I've no notion who it is. You've told me of Mr. Wingard and Mr. Dixon, but you haven't mentioned who the third was you managed to secure. I can't ask if I don't know."

"No. No, you can't." Her friend averted her gaze, colour riding high on her cheeks.

"Gwen." A sense of foreboding fell over her. She knew that look. Gwen had done something, something she knew Etta wouldn't like. "What have you done?"

"Nothing. I've done nothing. I've…" Her friend took a breath. "Well, you know how Edward loves

Gothic novels, and when I said I wanted to host guest speakers, he suggested I consider authors, and then he suggested I consider Gothic authors, and then he suggested Lord Christopher Hiddleston, and I couldn't say no to Edward, not when he is so very excited by the prospect, and it makes a lot of sense as Lord Christopher is quite famous and he will bring a large crowd, mostly of women, and they are the ones we wish to attend the school, and really it made a great deal of sense."

A deathly silence fell over the room.

Jaw tense, Etta finally said, "You said 'sense' twice."

A torrent of words fell from her friend. "I'm sorry I didn't tell you before, but I didn't know how. It's not the kind of thing one puts in a letter, and I didn't know if Lord Christopher would say yes, and by the time he did, which was only a fortnight ago, I was going to be travelling to Cambridge anyway, so I figured I'd just tell you in person, and you're being very quiet. Why are you being quiet?"

Etta couldn't speak. She didn't care that it caused Gwen concern, that her friend looked at her with pleading eyes. Gwen knew how she felt about that man. Why did the duke's wishes take precedence?

"Your Grace." The jovial butler stood in the door. "Lord Christopher Hiddleston's bags have been taken to his room, and he asks to see you."

A buzzing sounded in Etta's ears. No. No, he couldn't be staying here. Not where she herself had assumed she'd spend most of her time, as she had spent most of her time at the Parkes' house when they were growing up.

Colour high, her friend turned to the butler.

"Thank you, Henry. Please inform Lord Christopher I am indisposed and will see him at dinner."

The butler—Henry—bowed. "Yes, your Grace."

Silence again.

Teeth grinding, Etta forced herself to swallow. This was the one place where she was certain she would feel comfortable, where no one would think her peculiar or strange. When they were girls, she'd spent more time at the Parkes' than at her own home, the warmth of Mrs. Parkes' kitchen better than the cold silence of her father's table, Professor Parkes' willingness to discuss his lectures preferable to her father's exasperated refusals.

Now that was ruined because the bane of her existence was in attendance, invited by her dearest friend. The blow, doubled and intense, left her utterly without speech.

"Why is he staying with you?" she finally managed.

Gwen lifted a shoulder helplessly. "It seemed the thing to do."

"Did you know he still sends me articles?"

Her friend winced. "No."

"Well, he does." She exhaled. "I thought I would be able to stay here."

"You still can. Of course you can. There's more than enough room, and he's not so very bad, is he?"

That didn't even warrant a response.

Gwen looked miserable. "I could not say no. Edward… You should have seen how happy this made Edward."

Turning her head, she gazed at the wall and swallowed. She had no choice. Either she accepted Lord Christopher's presence here, or she could stay away, and she couldn't stay away. Gwen was here for a fortnight only, and those two weeks would go fast.

Slowly, she exhaled. She was a woman grown. She could pretend he didn't exist. "I understand."

"I shall keep him from you." A determined expression took Gwen's features. "With luck, you shall never have to see him."

"Yes. With luck." She forced a grin.

"Shall I ring for tea? I feel we should have some tea."

"Of course." Exhaling, she offered an olive branch. "And maybe share a Chelsea bun?"

Gwen visibly relaxed. "Oh, yes. Yes, definitely. Do you think the kitchen will have the ones from Bartells?" Her expression turned wistful. "I've not had one in an age."

Etta made a non-committal sound. They always shared a Chelsea bun after a disagreement, the fruit-filled treat a peace offering. "If they don't, I'm sure someone can be sent. After all, you are an important duchess-like person now. Don't people jump to do your bidding?"

"They do. It is most embarrassing."

"But desirous when Chelsea buns are in the equation."

"Oh yes. Anything for Chelsea buns."

The door banged, and they both jumped. The butler, Henry, stood in the doorway, his demeanour surprised, perturbed, and slightly afraid.

"Yes, Henry?" Gwen asked, showing no sign of noticing the error.

"Your Grace," the butler started, gratitude evident in his features. "There has been an incident."

Brows rising, Etta glanced between her friend and the butler. The man actually said it as if the word was capitalised.

Gwen frowned. "Can it not be handled by the staff?"

"No, your Grace. It has to do with"—the butler lowered his voice—"the special item from London."

How mysterious. Etta looked expectantly at Gwen for an explanation.

Which was not forthcoming. Her friend shot to her feet. "I'll attend to it right away." Halting, she glanced at Etta. "I'm sorry. It's important."

She waved her hand. "It's of no matter. Perhaps I shouldn't have come so soon after your arrival. I'll go home."

"No, please don't. I won't be long, I promise." Taking her hands, Gwen squeezed. "And I'm glad you came so soon. I should not have liked to have waited one second longer than necessary."

Warmth filled her, that her friend had clearly missed her just as much. "I shall stay."

"Good." Gwen rose. "I'll attend to this and be back before you know it."

She raised a brow haughtily. "Very well, but don't take too long. I'm extremely busy, you know."

At that, Gwen grinned. "I shan't."

After her friend departed, Etta rose from the chaise to wander idly. Making her way to the fireplace, she trailed her fingers over the figurines displayed on the mantel. Paint was missing in places, and a few of them were chipped. Maybe the house had already been furnished? It seemed a reasonable assumption. Gwen would be here two weeks, and it would be a shameful waste of money to purchase furniture for such a short stay—Although the short time frame hadn't stopped Gwen from inviting Christopher Hiddleston to stay.

Etta scowled at the faded wallpaper. Why would her friend do such a thing? She knew he was the bane of Etta's existence. When she was a girl, Etta had convinced Gwen to attend the local pub in search of debate on points of law. She knew students of the universities frequented The Havisham Arms, and it had been wonderful. Stimulating conversation, stirring debate, discussion of the law...well, they'd had such, once she'd browbeaten the students to overlook their sex. Then, Lord Christopher Hiddleston and his friends had arrived.

Lord Christopher agreed with nothing she'd said. In fact, he'd taken such ludicrous stances she couldn't contain herself, rising to higher and higher passion as his smug grin and completely incorrect suppositions drove her spare. It had been a happy day when he'd finally graduated, and she could rest easy knowing The Havisham Arms would be hers once more.

Then, one day, the articles had arrived.

With no sense of regularity, he'd sent her articles detailing his exploits. Sometimes months would go by without one, and then four would arrive in quick succession. At first, they described his appointment to a fellowship at London University, and the publishing of a work or two on tort law. Then, he'd started sending her snippets of some awful Gothic novel. Then, he'd revealed himself to be the novelist. And then, to make matters infinitely worse, he'd become a ridiculously famous and successful novelist.

And now...now he was to stay with Gwen.

"Miss Wilding-Marsh, what a pleasure. What an absolute pleasure."

The hair on her neck rose. No. It couldn't be. Ill

thoughts couldn't conjure the devil. Could they?

Shoulders tensed, she turned. Standing inside the room, his face wreathed in a lunatic grin, stood Lord Christopher Hiddleston.

Fury filled her, such that it stole her tongue. Wrenching her gaze from him, she stonily regarded the fireplace. Maybe, if she pretended he wasn't there, he wouldn't be.

However, she had never been lucky. "Miss Wilding-Marsh?"

Resolutely, she stared forward, though she was overwhelmingly aware of his presence. Lord, she wished it were socially acceptable for her to just plant him a facer. She even had some notion of how to do so, given she'd infiltrated Harcourt's Gymnasium last summer to discover exactly how men went about pummelling each other for fun.

"I say, Miss Wilding-Marsh?"

Damnation, he wasn't going away. With no other recourse, she turned.

He looked different. Ten years had passed, and with time's passage, the boy had become a man. Auburn curls tumbled wildly about his head, too long and untamed by any hint of pomade. Dark eyes glittered wickedly beneath straight brows, like the pools of Hades on a particularly evil day, while his aquiline nose led to a mouth far too sensuous for such an annoying man. His strong jaw showed a hint of red-gold stubble, and his cravat was skewwhiff as if it had taken a battering, of what she had no clue. His garments showed the same battering, the grey overcoat stretching his broad shoulders slightly wrinkled. He was a full head taller, and he used the difference in their heights to smirk down at her.

Something curled low in her belly. Damnation,

he had always been ridiculously handsome. Why had God seen fit to pair a contrary disposition with such an exterior?

Ignoring whatever was floating about her stomach—which could only be the result of something she ate—she said flatly, "Lord Christopher."

He didn't even bother to disguise his glee. "Such a greeting. I do believe I shall blush at its fulsome and effulgent nature. I trust you are well?"

"I am."

"You do appear in fine health. There's a bloom to your cheeks that is quite fetching."

She gritted her teeth. "Thank you."

"It's been simply an age since we've seen each other, Miss Wilding-Marsh. Tell me." Moving to the chaise, he seated himself. "How has the intervening time been?"

"Fine."

"Are you going to ask after me?"

Her jaw dropped. "Are you joking, sir?"

"No." He flicked at invisible lint on his lapel.

"Have you not sent me completely unsolicited articles for the better part of ten years?"

The corner of his mouth quirked. "Yes."

"I know all about you I care to know."

He stretched his arm over the back of the chaise. And then he smiled.

A fury that seemed reserved solely for him roared through her. Whipping to face the mantel, she took a deep breath. Good God, how could it be ten years since she'd seen him and yet he still had the power to drive her completely mental? It was irrational to feel this intense irritation for someone on the periphery of her life, and it was insane that he had the power to affect her, that his mere presence in Gwen's house forced a disagreement between her and her oldest friend.

He still regarded her, dark eyes dancing wickedly.

"Do you have anything of substance to impart?" she burst out.

A slow grin spread across his face. "Everything I say is of substance."

"Who told you that? The legions of sycophants who laughingly believe you a stalwart of literature?"

"My sycophants would never be so gauche as to refer to my work as literature," he said mildly. "Ah, Miss Wilding-Marsh, I do delight in our relationship. I've missed your invectives."

"What do you expect? You sent me those cursed articles for years and years, despite my frequent and passionate demands to cease. You, sir, are no gentleman."

"My title would seem to disagree."

"Your behaviour marks you no gentleman. It has nothing to do with an accident of birth."

"Ah. That old argument? It's almost as if we were again ensconced in The Havisham Arms. Well, Miss Wilding-Marsh, do continue. Tell me again how an accident of birth should not dictate the distribution of power and wealth."

He was laughing at her. She was certain of it. Counting to ten, she took a breath. And then another. And yet another. "I shall not engage you in debate, sir. I merely await the return of my friend while you are clearly frittering your time away on pointless endeavours of little interest and no weight."

He laughed. "I am delighted our repartee—our persiflage, if you will—remains as dexterous and adroit as ever, almost as if the years have never passed."

She crossed her arms. Did he think to confuse her with such language? She had made herself a student of the law, and there could be no greater challenge than to understand legal terminology. He could use all the ridiculously convoluted words he wished, and he would not confound her. "A true gentleman would leave me in peace."

"Ah, but then that true gentleman of yours would not have the pleasure of your company, and I find, Miss Wilding-Marsh, immense pleasure in your company."

She snorted.

A look of delight overtook his features. "Did you just snort, Miss Wilding-Marsh?

She refused to dignify that with an answer. "Why are you here?"

"In the room? It seemed a comfortable sort of room, and I was desirous of comfort."

She gritted her teeth. "No. In Cambridge."

"Ah." He leant back into the chaise. "I was invited."

It would be wrong to beat him about the head. Besides, he didn't need to know how much he annoyed her. "Why did you accept the invitation?"

One auburn brow rose. "Why wouldn't I?"

"Because this is Cambridge. Because few of your sycophantic readers would reside here. Because you are in support of a school for women."

"Why wouldn't I support a school for women?"

"I—" Her mind went blank. She had never thought he would support the education of women. There was no real reason for her supposition, apart from he'd always been contrary.

"I have always counted you to be the cleverest person of my acquaintance, especially about matters of law," he continued. "Why wouldn't I support the education of other similar women?"

Mind. Blank.

His gaze strayed to the clock on the mantel and then he rose to his feet. "Miss Wilding-Marsh, it has been, as I've said, a pleasure. I hope to repeat it soon." With a flourish and a bow, he departed.

Mouth agape, she stared after him. What... He just... Had he seriously just left? Abruptly and without explanation, after stirring her about? He was the most insolent, infuriating, annoying man...

She was still fuming five minutes later when Gwen reappeared, full of apologies and preceding Chelsea buns and tea. Worse, she still thought on him hours later, when she'd returned home and lay in bed, grinding her teeth over a devilish man with autumn-coloured hair and wicked dark eyes.

Chapter Two

LORD CHRISTOPHER HIDDLESTON LOATHED crowds. He disliked the press of bodies against his person. He abhorred the heat generated by too many in too small a space. He detested the necessity of raising one's voice, and he hated the cacophony that reverberated in one's ears.

Strangely, though, he loved public houses.

The Havisham Arms had not changed in the time from his last patronage to this, and considering the period had encompassed some years, that was quite a feat. Innocuously nestled between an apothecary and a printer's, The Havisham Arms had been the site of many a drunken revel, he and his university friends often cavorting within its hallowed halls. It was here, too, he'd argued with a certain passionate girl with carrot-coloured hair and a determined set to her jaw.

Lifting the pint glass, he took a draught. He hadn't had Golden Cam Ale since he was a student, but the taste was the same, as everything was the same since last he'd been in Cambridge, and he needed the beer after the day he'd had.

The reading had gone well, better than even he had expected. The crowd had been enthralled, hanging upon his every word and giving him every confidence *The Manse* would be well received upon its publication next month. There had been the usual mix of persons: those from the literary crowd who sat with arms crossed, ready to decry his work as populous nonsense, though they were small in number; those who hung on his every word as if spellbound, applauding furiously at every pause in the reading while they juggled packages that looked suspiciously like volumes of his novels tucked in their laps. And there were the young ladies, those who giggled and seemed taken with what he knew to be his more than decent appearance. Vanity, it was true, but he'd lived with himself for twenty-eight years. He saw his face in the mirror every day, and he knew it to be pleasing to members of the opposite sex.

A wave of exhaustion swept him, sudden and intense. Bloody hell, it always hit him fast after one of his readings. He loved it in the moment, the rush of sharing his work, the thrill of watching the dawn of delight on his audience's faces, and it was never until it was over and done that his body reminded him such a high sapped him of all strength. Always he was taken by surprise, even though it happened every single time.

This afternoon, he'd been succeeded by an adventure novelist. The adventure novelist—he couldn't remember his name for the life of him—had read a passage on someone becoming shipwrecked on an uninhabited island. He supposed the adventure novel was all well and good but it wasn't his particular cup of tea. His bread and butter was the Gothic novel, that strange beast of horror and romance. His latest put his intrepid heroine in mortal peril on a regular basis, such that one could almost query why she continued to inhabit the home of the dark and brooding baron, the titular manse of the title. However, after countless dangers and near misses, the heroine solved the mystery of the manse, won the love of the misunderstood baron, and lived happily ever after. The good ended happily and the bad unhappily and all was again right with the world.

The corner of his mouth lifted. If only real life occurred in the same way.

In real life, though, he had little to complain about. His novels were insanely popular, which lead to him being insanely wealthy and therefore independent from his brother. The earl would huff and splutter about his vastly younger brother's predilection but had no way of enforcing his displeasure.

A commotion from the bar drew his attention. A university student berated the barkeep, his wildly gesticulating hands indicating the decreased level of his sobriety. Christ, a dozen years ago, that could have been him.

Bored by the display, he allowed his gaze to wander. The usual suspects inhabited the pub—the older gents who would brag to anyone who listened, the shop girls from the local drapery's, the family from out of town looking for a bite to eat. No one out of the ordinary, or of interest.

The door to the pub opened and Miss Henrietta Wilding-Marsh stood in the entranceway, windswept and red faced.

A great rush filled him, and he sat straighter in his chair. He hadn't expected to meet Henrietta Wilding-Marsh so soon upon his arrival, had in fact expected it would take days before he tracked her down and before he came up with the perfect way to re-enter her life. How serendipitous their next meeting took just as little effort as the first. It was like the universe wanted them to meet.

She removed her bonnet, revealing a wild tangle of carrot-red hair. How she'd managed that, he had no clue. Weren't bonnets supposed to protect a lady's hair? However, it had never been in control the entire time he'd known her, always rioting about her head like a haystack, and his fingers itched to tug a strand, as they always had. Just once, he wished he had. She would scowl, her brown eyes spitting fire and disdain at him, and the exhilaration her response caused would tempt him to do it again.

He found her completely and utterly fascinating.

From the moment she had first stormed up to him in The Havisham Arms and started lambasting him, he hadn't been able to look away. He used to love that he could rile her to passion with not much more than a sentence. If he were being honest, he still loved it. It was why he'd sought her out yesterday, why he'd insisted upon keeping her company while she awaited the duchess in direct opposition to the good manners his mother had installed in him.

Ten years was a long time to be fascinated, especially when the majority of it had been spent apart, but Etta inspired that kind of devotion. He thought of her as Etta, the familiar the Duchess of Sowrith used, and he was certain she would be furious if she knew he thought of her thus. For years, he'd sent her any and all articles of him the newssheets had run, and he'd even sent her his writing when he'd been reluctant to show it to anyone.

His brows drew. Why had he done that? He'd sent her those snippets with no explanation, and he'd continued even after she'd given him yet another set down, though at the time she hadn't known he was the author. He'd honed his craft on her comments, taking her criticism and turning his work into something that approached readable. Even now, she was the first person he thought to show his work, though he restrained himself. Most of the time.

Getting to his feet, he made his way towards her. Anticipation increased with every step. By the time he got to her, by the time she'd noticed and rolled her eyes before squaring her shoulders defiantly, it was a steady thrum in his veins.

He smiled genially. "Miss Wilding-Marsh."

He should not be so delighted by the look of disgust her features formed, as if she smelled something particularly rotten. "Lord Christopher," she said flatly.

Ah, still disgruntled by his presence. How splendid. "It's a delight to see you again in our old stomping ground. Not much has changed."

She crossed her arms. "What do you want?"

Her scowl was a thing of beauty. "The pleasure of your company, of course."

"Well, you cannot have such a thing. I have better things to do than to engage in discourse with such as you."

He made a show of glancing about them. "Truly? What, pray tell, could possible compare?"

Exhaling forcefully, she said, "I've come to seek my supper, not argue with you."

And yet, she made no move toward the dining room. "I'm not stopping you."

"How can I possibly eat when you block my way?"

Stepping aside, he offered a flourishing bow. "Miss Wilding-Marsh, I should never stand in the way of a lady and food."

Lifting her chin, she brushed past him.

He followed her.

She shot him a glare. "What are you doing?"

"I also require supper. What a happy coincidence. Shall we dine together? After all, it is unseemly for a lady to dine alone." He wasn't sure it was particularly proper for a lady to dine with a gentleman to whom she was not related, but he wasn't going to mention it.

"I-I don't believe—" Consternation crossed her features as she clearly couldn't think of an excuse. "I thank you, yes," she finally said, though her expression clearly stated she wished no such thing.

Holding out his arm, he said, "Shall we?"

Reluctantly, she looped her arm with his.

The dining room was half full, mainly university students and a few families. They found a table, made their order, and then she proceeded to ignore him, determinedly looking from him.

He studied her profile. What was it he found so fascinating? Her appearance was all that was ordinary, regular features with no particular claim to beauty, and she was altogether too short, at least a foot less than him by his reckoning. She wore clothes two years out of date, regarded one with an intensity that was almost painful at times, took everything literally, and was overwhelmingly passionate for causes others disdained. And, of course, he couldn't forget she seemed to take particular delight in arguing with every single thing he said. She did possess character, that stalwart quality he found more interesting than appearance, however he should have forgotten her as soon as he left Cambridge. Nothing about her should compel his fascination...but when she directed her ire, her passion, he found her incandescent.

It was odd she sought her supper at the local pub. By his recollection, she possessed a father and a home. Surely, she should be dining with her parent?

Finally, she must have become sick of his perusal. "What?"

Leaning forward, he said, "What do you think of my books?" He'd always wondered.

Her expression remained unimpressed. "I have better things to do with my time than converse upon your books."

"I'm most desirous of your opinion, Miss Wilding-Marsh," he said, as if he didn't care one way or the other.

"I shall tell you the truth," she warned.

"I expect nothing less."

"Your books are populous nonsense, shrewdly aimed at the lowest common denominator. They have no redeeming feature, no greater meaning, no commentary on the world at large."

He allowed false delight to colour his expression. "You think I'm *shrewd*?"

She rolled her eyes. "You would pick out the vaguest of compliments. I cannot think why anyone should read such."

"And yet, thousands do." Possibly more, but he was above all things a modest soul.

"It is as I said. Populous nonsense."

"And what would you have the general public read? Huge, dry tomes on tort law and its relevance to

19th century lawmaking?" he asked.

"Only for those who are interested. Why cannot you write something of more meaning? If you must write populous claptrap, at least write the *best* populous claptrap."

"Have you read my work?"

"Out of curiosity. And a sense of deep self-punishment." She shook her head. "You have talent, I'll grant you that, but you waste it on base clichés and tired stereotypes."

He honestly didn't know whether to be flattered or insulted. He certainly wasn't hurt. The books he wrote were claptrap, and he knew it. He'd deliberately aimed low, and it seemed his public was determined to keep him there. It was the bed he'd made, and now he must lie in it.

Never had he thought to make a career of it. It had been nothing more than scribbles, bits and pieces of story he'd jotted down between descriptions of ancient laws and codicils. Then one day, when he was feeling a particular kind of hubris, he'd gathered the scribbles, put them in some semblance of order, and sent them to a publisher.

It had surprised him as much as anyone when the publisher had offered him a deal. A twelve-part Gothic serial, which had somehow captured the imagination of London. Before he knew it, he'd published three novels and become something of a phenomenon.

His brother had been horrified, of course, not that the earl ever had overtly displayed such. The earl had said little, as he always did, but he'd called Christopher to his study, as if he were again a lad and his much-older brother was taking him to task. The earl had outlined in stiff and formal tones the notoriety and disdain Christopher had brought to the Hiddleston name and it would be in the best interest of all if he quit this rebellion and took his proper place again at the university. His path was scholarly, and then political.

He'd stood, listened, and promptly ignored him, much as he had when a lad.

His mother had laughed when he'd first told her, and then she'd gaily claimed she'd always known he would lean towards the creative. He'd told her of the earl's reaction, and she'd dismissed her stepson as high-handed and overly concerned with the inconsequential. If Christopher wished to be a Gothic novelist, well he was a Hiddleston. He could do as he pleased.

His sisters revelled in the fact their younger brother was a Gothic novelist, loftily informing their friends *they* had read the next chapter of his latest book before any other. And now his novels had brought him back to Cambridge, to sit here with Etta Wilding-Marsh who wore a scowl and studiously looked at anything but him.

Their meals arrived. He waited until she'd taken her first bite before saying, "So which of my books did you read?"

She choked on her food, her eyes watering as she swallowed. Pointing her fork at him, she glared. "I do not wish to discuss this any further."

"But you have fired my curiosity, Miss Wilding-Marsh. You have read one of my books, and I simply won't be able to rest until I know which one. Was it *Miranda of the Moors*? Or *The Black Count*? No, it must be *The Fisherman's Ode*. Tell me, was it *The Fisherman's Ode*?"

She shuddered. "Dear God, they are terrible

titles."

"They are, aren't they? Ah well, they were my publisher's idea." He snapped his fingers. "It was *The Secret of Bleckfell Hall.*"

"If you must know, I read your serial, along with the rest of the country." She took a mouthful of beef.

Ha. As if her consuming food would stop him. "Ah. The serial. That which set me upon this present path."

"Yes. We have so much to thank it for." The disgust in her voice was music to his ears. "But I have no wish to speak of this further."

"Then what shall we discuss?"

"Nothing. Eat your supper."

He ignored her. "The finer points of law? Perhaps the decisions made over the last year in reference to *Regina v. Boak* and how it affects the common man."

"As if you'd know anything. You're not even a professor."

"Incorrect. I hold a fellowship at London University. I sometimes drop by, to chew the fat as it were."

Her jaw dropped. Silence reigned while she undertook a fair impression of a fish. "You don't even know what you have, do you?" she finally managed.

"On the contrary, I know very well." He smiled beatifically. "I have a fellowship."

Mouth agape, eyes wide, she looked completely flummoxed. Good. He enjoyed flummoxing her.

"I cannot—" She took a breath, as if to bring back a measure of calm. "I cannot believe you treat a fellowship with such casualty, as if it is a thing easily obtained and of no value."

Uncomfortable of a sudden, he maintained his smile.

"Many wish for what you have gained so easily, for what you now throw away," she continued, eyes blazing. "Many more cannot even aspire to it. *I* cannot aspire to it. It is something I will never achieve. There is nothing more I want in this life than to live the law, to catalogue it, teach it, argue its merits, and yet, merely because I am born female, this is denied me. Then you have the unmitigated *gall* to joke and dismiss such a thing as if it is nothing." Disdain was writ large on her features. "Is it any wonder I dislike you?"

A deathly sort of silence fell over the table.

Stomach like lead, Christopher balled his hands on the table. He had miscalculated. Her expression didn't hold the usual scowl of annoyance, the one that encouraged him to keep pushing. If anything, her expression boarded on disgust—*actual* disgust.

She pushed her plate from her. "I find I have lost my appetite."

Bloody hell, how had it gone so wrong so quickly? He racked his brain for something, anything, to change the tone. He wanted her annoyed, not angry. Not disgusted. "I apologise, Miss Wilding-Marsh. I did not think—"

Placing her napkin on top of her plate, she rose from the table. "Good evening, Lord Christopher."

He shot to his feet. "What? No. I didn't mean—Miss Wilding-Marsh, Etta, please—"

She looked him direct. "You could be better, you know." Dark-brown eyes held him. "I have read your books. You possess a pleasing turn of phrase, and your prose is not terrible. You have more in you than tales of brainless women without a thought in their heads finding themselves in constant peril and the milquetoasts who rescue them. As it is, your writing is lazy and trite, and you are capable of more." She paused. Further, you know this, and still, you do not try. Good evening, Lord Christopher."

He stared after her as she departed. She was right. Of course she was right. He did coast. He wrote the same story over and over because it was what worked. He had ideas, other stories in him that pushed and prodded and fairly demanded to be told, but those were untried, untested, and if he failed...if he failed...

Shaking himself, he sat back at his meal, picking up his cutlery and sawing at his steak. What did Etta Wilding-Marsh know? He'd not seen her in ten years, and she'd applied herself to being aloof and argumentative the entire time. Her opinion held no weight.

He exhaled, his hand tightening on his fork. Who was he trying to fool? Her opinion held weight.

It always had.

Chapter Three

SCULLS SLICED THROUGH THE Cam, arrowing towards the finish with grace and speed. The calm call of the coxes belied the efforts of the team, the rowers forcing the oars through the dragging water in unison to propel the boats to the finish.

On the banks of the Cam, Etta bobbed on her toes, fighting to see over those standing before her. The crowd on the shore barracked and cheered, the men and women around her shaking fists at their opposition and yelling encouragement at their team.

Cursing, she wavered unsteadily on the balls of her feet. Gwen should be here, but, instead, Etta stood here by herself, cheering by herself. Every year, Gwen would come home from London for May Week, and they would attend the end of university year functions they were invited to and, more enjoyably, the ones to which they weren't. Of course, Gwen would protest, but Etta would convince her of the fun they would have, and Gwen would always cave.

And they would attend the boat races. They would watch from the banks of the Cam, yelling encouragement at the Cambridge lads and booing the enemy Oxford as they rowed past. Last year, Gwen had been in Devon and unable to attend. This year, though, she was in Cambridge but still could not attend. Apparently, her husband had need of her.

Etta kicked at the ground. She never saw Gwen anymore. Her friend always cancelled, or she was busy, or she forgot, and they only had two weeks before she returned to Dartmoor.

Swallowing, Etta set her jaw as she watched the boats. The fellow before her cheered, waving his arms in the air and obscuring her view further. He was a giant of man, at least a head taller than she, and clearly possessed no sense of consideration.

She poked him in the shoulder. The man whirled around, brows drawn. Clearly expecting another giant, he lowered his gaze when he discovered instead her.

"Sir, I ask you be aware of those around you. Some of us are not freakishly tall," she said.

The man's scowl darkened. "Maybe you should position yourself toward the front. Especially seeing as you're freakishly short."

She narrowed her eyes. "I can stand wherever I wish. Furthermore, I cannot make my way to the front as it is a sad crush. However, this is neither here nor there as I have just as much right as the next person to stand wherever I wish, without the obstruction of a behemoth of a man completely unaware of his surrounds standing before me and—"

"Miss Wilding-Marsh, what an absolute delight to see you again."

She whirled around. Lord Christopher Hiddleston stood there, somehow unaffected by the push of the crowd, grinning his stupidly handsome grin at her.

Why? Why was she so cursed?

After the evening before last, she thought to be done with him. His flippancy regarding his fellowship had infuriated her, more so than usual. She stewed on it for longer than she wished, and she couldn't erase the image of his stricken expression as he stumbled through an abortive apology. He'd called her Etta, and, for some reason, his use of the familiar only Gwen used didn't offend. She'd found herself softening, even as she told herself he didn't deserve her forgiveness. It was *him*, after all, the man who had plagued her all these years.

But she couldn't erase his stricken expression.

"Is she yours?" The tall man hooked a thumb at her.

Etta glared at the imbecile. "I am no one's, sir, but my own."

He held his hands up, his gaze well over her head. "You've your hands full with that one, mate."

Lord Christopher's expression remained mild, but his eyes hardened. "Miss Wilding-Marsh is, as she says, her own. I in no way influence her behaviour, but I must find myself in agreeance with her assertion."

The man shrugged and turned back to the racing. And still blocked her view.

Etta transferred her glare to the man beside her. "I didn't need your help."

Lord Christopher's brow rose. "I wasn't aware I offered it."

"I was handling that man quite well on my own."

"I completely agree."

"It was of no use anyway. This man is clearly

an inconsiderate lout." She raised her voice at the last.

The man ignored her, discounting her complaint as so many of his sex did.

"Swap places with me," Lord Christopher said.

"Pardon?"

"Swap places with me." Taking her arm, he urged her to his spot.

"There is no need for such—" Damnation, now she had the perfect view. Well, never let it be said she couldn't be gracious when the situation warranted. "Thank you."

He gave a little half-smile. Ignoring how it made her shiver, she returned her contemplation to the race.

For one glorious moment, he was silent. Then, "Is it annoying being so short?"

She wasn't going to answer that, even though she'd just been lamenting the same thing. "Do you absolutely have to fill every silence?"

He thought about it for a moment. "You know, I believe I do. So, is it?"

"Is it what?"

"Annoying being short."

"Yes," she said with finality, and hoped that was the end of the matter.

That, it seemed, was the answer he required. He fell silent, his gaze on the boats slicing through the Cam.

She couldn't help glancing at him. His strong profile lured her time and again, and if she didn't know his character, she would admit she found his appearance fascinating. She grimaced. Lord, how very lowering. She was swayed by a pretty face.

Turning his head, he caught her staring. He

gave a little smile.

Quickly, she averted her gaze back to where it should be. Two boats raced neck and neck, veritable leagues ahead of the other contenders, but she couldn't remain silent. "Why are you here?"

"To watch the races, of course." She could hear the amusement in his voice.

Through gritted teeth, she said, "No, why are you *here*?"

"Ah. Much clearer."

She took a deep breath. *Calm, Etta.* "One…two…" she muttered under her breath.

"Are you counting to ten?" Definitely amusement in his words.

She ignored him. Upon reaching ten, she said, "Why have you returned to Cambridge? You never have before."

"How do you know? It could be I've returned and you didn't know of it."

"It could be. But it isn't."

His expression displayed fascination. "I'm not even going to ask how you know."

Raising her brows, she waited.

"The duchess asked me," he finally said.

"That can't be the only reason."

He shrugged.

Gah, he drove her *insane*. He never answered as he should, and his responses were always unfathomable, yet when he pursued a line of questioning, he kept at her until she couldn't help but retort.

Someone shoved into her. Stumbling, she raised her hand, catching herself on his chest. He steadied her with his own hand at the small of her back, a glare directed at the person who jostled her.

Her breath caught. Cloth covering hard muscle lay under her palm, while his hand warmed her through the layers of clothing at her back. He was strong, so much stronger than she expected, not that she knew what to expect. She'd never touched a man's chest before, and to have it be his... Something curled low in her belly, something warm and peculiar, and she felt flushed, more so than the crush of the crowd warranted.

Wetting her lips, she slowly raised her gaze. He looked over the top of her head, ire shaping his expression.

"Bloody crowds." Focussing on her, he dropped his hand from her back. "Are you well?"

Reality came crashing, returning in a rush. Averting her eyes, she snatched her hand from him. "Yes. Yes, I'm fine."

"Are you blushing?"

Clenching her fists, she resisted the urge to cover her cheeks. "No."

"Are you certain? You appear decidedly red."

"Well, I'm not." She glanced away. The race was over, but she barely took note, the cheers from the crowd a dull roar in her ears. Lord above, what was she thinking? He was attractive, yes, she had to concede that, but he wasn't attractive to *her*. He annoyed her, he infuriated her, he'd sent her articles for over ten years just to keep her aggravation at a constant boil. Any surface attraction could not take precedence over that behaviour, and now he was here, still annoying her, still aggravating her... She frowned. But why?

She studied him a moment longer, carefully turning over the question in her mind. "Why *have* you come to Cambridge? Now, and not next week or next year."

His grin slowly died. Then, a devil lit in his eyes, and he drew in breath.

She held up her hand. "The truth, for once."

For a moment, he seemed as if he would protest, then he shrugged. "I have a novel that will be published next month. The duchess asked me to be a part of her tour. I thought to visit my old stomping ground." He grinned. "You were here."

She raised an eyebrow. "And I am such a drawcard?"

"You've always been a drawcard. You get a frown between your brows, right here." He indicated the space between his brows. "It is most amusing."

"You are decidedly odd. You know that, don't you?"

His reply was merely to grin.

She crossed her arms. She didn't believe anything he said, not for a moment. The warmth she felt when first she heard his words, like champagne bubbles in her chest, was the result of too much sun, nothing more. "You are truly a supporter of the school?"

"Of course."

It was too unbelievable. "Of course," she echoed

Something she supposed was amusement played with his expression. "My sisters were envious when I left for Cambridge. They had governesses, and of course my mother ensured their education was wider than the pianoforte and watercolours, but it's not the same as attending university. I should have liked to have argued with them in tutorials."

Surprise filled her. "You have sisters?"

"I even have a mother. I didn't climb out from

under a rock. I have a family."

Chastised, she closed her mouth. A sudden roar from the crowd drew her attention to the river as she processed that information. He was the younger brother of Earl Hiddleston, but she'd not thought of him having a family, sisters who teased him, a mother who loved him.

A small smile played about his finely moulded lips. "Do you wish to know of them?"

A torrent of words fell from her. "How many sisters do you have? How old are they? What do they think of your novels? Do they believe you've wasted your time at university?"

"Three. I would never be so foolish as to reveal a lady's age, and most definitely not my sisters'. They have differing opinions of my books and debate them spiritedly. No."

She absorbed this information. "And your mother? What does she think?"

"She loves me."

"What does that have to do with anything?"

His brows drew. "Everything."

Exhaling forcefully, she crossed her arms. His responses were ridiculous. "What kind of answer is that?"

"The only one I have." His hand twitched, and she had the oddest feeling he wanted to touch her, perhaps her arm. He didn't, though. "My mother wishes me to be content, happy, as she wishes the same for her daughters, in whatever form that takes. If I choose an incorrect path along the way, she will not hold me at fault for that."

Brows drawing, she bit her lip. What he described was beyond her experience. Well, her personal experience. Gwen's parents seemed to hold her in a similar regard. "And your sisters truly do not hold ire that your time at Cambridge counted for little to nothing?"

"It didn't count for nothing. I made friends who are still amongst those closest to me. I took a course that led directly to my becoming published." The corner of his mouth lifted. "I met you."

Quickly, she turned her attention to the races. His tone had been casual, as if his words meant nothing, so of course they didn't.

She could feel him watching her, his regard almost like a warm touch upon her skin, and she couldn't help thinking that maybe they did mean something. But what? They had never been friends. Indeed, combatants would be more accurate. Maybe he was being flippant, or maybe she was treating his words with more consideration than they deserved. And why was she standing here with him? There were any number of places she could watch the races…but then, she would *not* allow him to chase her from *this* place. He had joined her. He could be the one to leave.

Determinedly, she proceeded to ignore his presence at her side. He didn't speak, but he glanced at her every now and then, his expression warm and open and…confusing to her. Then, finally, when the races were done, she bid him a polite farewell and made her way home, leaving him and confusion behind.

Chapter Four

THE PROFUSION OF LILACS peppering the meeting hall was giving Christopher a headache. Surreptitiously, he rubbed his eyes, hoping the action would magically clear the irritation from his head. No such luck. Instead, it made his eyes ache all the more. However, he had chosen to take refuge here amongst the flowers, and he would damn well put up with itchy eyes and a runny nose for five minutes of peace.

Rubbing his eyes again, he exhaled. Damn, but he disliked England in May. His entire university career, he'd had to pretend he enjoyed the festivities the end of the scholarly year brought, but, for him, it was red eyes, running nose, and a stuffed head. Others may have enjoyed the endless balls and assemblies, the rowing on the Cam, and pummelling each other at rugby, but he'd just been in the corner, quietly trying not to die. How joyous to discover nothing had changed.

He gave up attempting to make his eyes feel as if they belonged to a human. He would just have to persevere, and if any commented...well, he was a writer. Surely he could make something up more scintillating than "plants are trying to kill me".

Pretending idleness, he watched the entrance. The duke and duchess still welcomed guests, both appearing vaguely ill-at-ease. The duke leaned heavily on his right leg, his left side slightly angled from those greeting him. It was obvious why. The duke was scarred, and it had become apparent to Christopher within twenty minutes of meeting the duke that his Grace was painfully conscious of that fact. He would often turn so his unscarred side was prominent, angling his head so the patch covering where his left eye should have been was hidden.

The duke had been comically excited to make Christopher's acquaintance. He could tell the man was usually a taciturn sort, quiet and withdrawn, but his love of Gothic literature made him animated, expounding at length upon Christopher's work and its place amongst the classics. While he was more than happy to accept such praise, he knew his writing of late was mediocre at best. On that, Etta Wilding-Marsh had been correct.

As for the duchess, she had, until her marriage, been Miss Parkes, a commoner with no connection to the aristocracy. She did her best to seem welcoming and comfortable, but every now and then, it was apparent her new position overwhelmed her.

Leaning against a wall, he considered the duchess. He'd always liked her, back when she'd been Miss Gwendolyn Parkes and she'd sat in The Havisham Arms, nursing a lemonade and concealing a grin as her friend had argued with him. It had been almost serendipitous when he'd received an invitation from the Duke of Sowrith to stay as the duke's guest while in Cambridge.

Crossing his arms, he kept his gaze on the

entrance. Still no familiar mop of carrot-red hair atop a furious scowl. He set his jaw. He knew she was coming. The duchess had let that information slip, though she'd immediately looked as if she wished she'd instead swallowed her tongue.

"Lord Christopher." An eager young man and an equally eager young woman approached, and, judging by the similarity of their features, they could only be siblings.

Adopting a genial smile, Christopher pushed himself from the wall. "Good evening, sir. I don't believe we've been introduced."

"No. No, indeed we haven't," the young man said, his face almost split with his grin. "I am Oliver Wolton and this is my sister, Miss Maria Wolton." He bowed sharply while his sister executed a fine curtsy.

Christopher returned the gesture. "A delight to meet you, Mr. Wolton, Miss Wolton. Are you enjoying the ball?"

"Oh yes." Miss Wolton fairly vibrated with excitement. "I am so, so pleased to make the acquaintance of the duke and duchess, and of course, of yourself. I have read all your novels. *All* of them."

"I am flattered, Miss Wolton."

"I have read them, too, Lord Christopher," Mr. Wolton interjected. "I am particularly enamoured of *The Spires of Windfell Hall*."

Amused, Christopher said, "A particular favourite of mine, too, Mr. Wolton. I am ecstatic you agree."

A delighted smile overtook Mr. Wolton's face, and he launched into a monologue, espousing his favourite quotes and passages. His sister added comments, clutching her brother's arm excitedly.

What else could Christopher do but listen? It

was truly a marvel his stories affected people in such a manner. Who would have thought words upon a page could engender such excitement? Maybe his stories were silly and trite, maybe they didn't reach the lofty heights of grand literature as some people said, but they made the Woltons happy.

He glanced at the entrance. The duke and duchess still greeted guests.

"I've always thought Esmerelda should have her own story. She was quite my favourite character. Have you any thoughts in that direction, Lord Christopher?" Miss Wolton waited expectantly.

Christopher snapped back to attention. "Esmerelda from *Raven Close*? I had not thought to write a story where she is the heroine, but it is an idea."

Miss Wolton nodded enthusiastically. "Oh yes, she would be *amazing*. She could enter the employ of Lord Raven's nephew, who is undoubtedly as mysterious as Lord Raven himself, and encounter a mystery, just as Hermione did. And they would, of course, fall in love and end happily." She sighed blissfully, while her brother nodded his emphatic agreement.

"Of course," he murmured. Had his work really become so predictable?

He glanced at the entrance, and then his whole being was arrested, thoughts of predictability fleeing.

Etta had arrived.

Holding her friend's hands, she talked animatedly as the duchess laughed in response. Her red hair was already coming loose, and her gown was an uninspired and indeterminate pastel colour, far too dull for the vibrant woman it contained.

It hit him then, like it always did, a solid whack

to his chest that hadn't lessened in all the years he'd known her, and it confounded him like it always did. She wasn't beautiful, didn't dress with anything approaching fashion, and was more likely to scowl at him than to smile, yet his fool heart sped at the sight of her. It had to be anticipation. Their conversations—he grinned—their *discussions* had always affected him thus.

The duchess gestured, and Etta followed her gaze. A frown immediately took residence on her features as their gazes locked, drawing her incongruously dark brows together. Was it wrong he felt such exhilaration at her ire? If nothing else, it meant she wasn't ignoring him.

He shifted, uncomfortable with the thought of her indifference.

"Are you acquainted with Miss Wilding-Marsh, Lord Christopher?"

Miss Wolton. This woman's brows were also drawn, only this time in a perplexed manner. "A little."

"She is most peculiar. I should say she doesn't like your work. At all."

Christopher bit back a retort. "What makes you say that?"

"She always has opinions to the contrary of everyone else. She does not do anything she should. Only look, she arrives alone. I am surprised at her nerve."

Mr. Wolton nodded his agreement. "She is well known for her peculiarities. She is not a proper sort of woman. Why, only last month she attempted to again attend a public lecture at King's College."

"Is she not a member of the public?" He would not condemn the boy out of hand. Perhaps he meant something different to what he had inferred.

"It was on the law." Mr. Wolton lowered his voice. "The *law*. Women should not attend such things."

"I see," he said, baring his teeth in an approximation of a smile. It seemed he had been correct in his initial assessment. His gaze wandered back to Etta. Would that he could make it so she could attend whatever lecture she wanted.

She said something to the duchess, and then she started toward him with a determined stride. His heart leapt. Anticipation began a thrum in his veins as she drew nearer, her scowl intensifying with each step. "Lord Christopher," she said in a clear voice.

Beside him, Miss Wolton gasped, but he didn't take his gaze from Etta. *He* had no qualms she approached without a proper introduction. "Miss Wilding-Marsh."

She ignored his greeting. "I received your missive."

Adrenalin spiked through him. When he'd seen the article in the local newspaper, he couldn't resist. "How delightful. The English postal system is truly a marvel."

She scowled. "What do you think you're about? I *know* you are in Cambridge. I do not require an article sent to me detailing that fact."

"You'll agree, though, it was extremely well written? I will offer my thanks to the author when next we cross paths."

Annoyance set her jaw. Deliberately, she turned her attention to the Woltons. "Maria. Mr. Wolton. Good evening."

Christopher concealed a grin.

"Good evening, Miss Wilding-Marsh," Mr.

Wolton mumbled.

"You are as bold as ever, Henrietta Wilding-Marsh," Miss Wolton announced in a high, tight voice. "You enter the ballroom alone and then introduce yourself to Lord Christopher. Have you no sense of propriety?"

"I don't have a brother to squire me about, Maria. If I don't do it myself, it will never get done."

Miss Wolton's breath exploded. "Oh, you are contrary, Henrietta Wilding-Marsh! Will you not think of those around you, who are simply *scandalised* by your boldness? Lord Christopher is used to the quality of London, and you will have him believe we are little better than savages."

Etta tilted her head, expressionless. "Savages, Maria? Are we sinking to exaggeration?"

"I find Miss Wilding-Marsh's lack of pretention charming," Christopher interjected.

Two pairs of eyes shot him daggers. Being a wise man occasionally, he fell silent. Clearly, this enmity between the two women was of a long standing and had little to do with him.

"It is not an exaggeration," Miss Wolton announced. "You flout the rules of society as if they mean nothing."

"They mean little, it is true. They do nothing more than rigidly structure and bind our sex with pointless adherence to outmoded rituals. I should expect nothing less from you, as a proponent of outdated mores."

Miss Wolton turned a rather alarming shade of red. "Oliver, I wish to partake of the lemonade," she announced and, taking her startled brother's arm, swept past them.

Etta scowled after her.

Christopher cleared his throat. Brown eyes swung to regard him, and now she wore her scowl for him. "That was entertaining."

"Oh, be quiet." She drummed her fingers against her skirts.

Obligingly, he did so, watching as she stewed. Finally, she sighed, her gaze wandering to the duchess, and he knew as if her thoughts were his own she meant to leave.

Racking his brain, he tried to think of something to make her stay. The strains of a minuet started, and inspiration struck.

Bowing low, he held out his hand. "Miss Wilding-Marsh, may I have the pleasure of this dance?"

Her gaze whipped to his. "I beg your pardon?"

Smiling as charmingly as he could, he said, "May I have the pleasure of this dance?"

A different type of frown settled on her brow. He would deem this one "confusion." "Why?"

"Because I wish to dance with you, and hope you wish the same."

Still frowning, she said, "I should say yes, just so I can step all over your feet."

He began to feel a bit like an idiot, holding out his hand, but he persevered. "I am reputed to be an excellent dancer."

"But I am not."

Of course Etta would baldly state she wasn't a good dancer. "Why is that?"

"It is difficult to refine one's skill when one is not asked." She said it matter-of-factly and showed no sign her lack of partners affected her in any way. Why was it, then, that he thought perhaps it had?

"I will take the chance my feet will be trampled.

Please." Hoping for a persuasive tone, he lowered his voice. "Dance with me."

Her eyes widened. The ball around them faded, until all he could see were uncertain brown eyes, ready to retreat at the first hint of insincerity.

Finally, cautiously, she took his hand. Slender fingers curled about his, clothed in plain white cotton. Her palm was narrow, delicate, and dwarfed by his. For a fleeting moment, he wished his gloves and hers gone, wished he could feel the slide of her skin against his.

Shaking his head, he dismissed the thought as he led her to the dance floor, taking position opposite her in the row of dancers. The first steps of the dance brought them close, her head barely brushing his chin, her shoulders narrow. So odd to think of Etta as delicate. She possessed such fire, held such passionate opinions, that one almost forgot she was really a tiny dab of a person.

They danced for a time in silence, long enough for him to notice the slight fragrance of honeysuckle and violets. Her hair. Her hair smelt of honeysuckle and violets.

"My father wishes to invite you to dinner Thursday next," she said suddenly.

He started, telling himself he wasn't trying to enjoy more of that elusive scent. Instead, he concentrated on her words. He vaguely remembered Professor Wilding-Marsh from his studies, a taciturn man who had bored them with tort law. The professor's comprehensive readings were legendary, and he could only imagine Etta's vast knowledge of case law came in part from her father. The rest, of course, would have derived from her dogged persistence and inability to comply with Society's expectations that she act as a woman ought. He'd always found such limitations baffling—Etta was a woman, so however she acted was as a woman ought. His own mother and sisters did as they pleased and were happier for it.

The thought of his own parent drew a question about hers. "Why is your father not here?"

Her brow creased. "Why would he be here?"

"Because you are his daughter and you have attended. The bounds of etiquette and good manners would suggest he escort you."

"I can escort myself. Besides, he dislikes social gatherings with no intellectual merit."

"So, he never attends, takes no interest?"

"No."

How strange. He couldn't comprehend his mother not taking an interest in his movements. Even now, though he was a man grown, she accompanied him to events in London, attended his signings, and bullied her sisters into doing the same.

The dance finished. Executing the sharpest bow he could, he grinned. "Miss Wilding-Marsh, how delightful. You didn't step on my toes once."

Her curtsey wobbled, and when she rose, that familiar scowl furrowed her brow. "You, sir, are, as I've said many, many times, no gentleman."

"A sad state of affairs, to be sure," he said genially.

"And one I no longer care to endure. I thank you for the dance. Good evening." She curtseyed again and departed, heading straight for the duchess.

He watched her go, wearing now his own frown. She did that too often. Leaving him. Maybe he would come up with a way to make it so she found it difficult to do so.

He deliberately didn't ask himself why it was so important she stay by his side.

Chapter Five

CHRISTOPHER SPREAD HIS LEGS as much as the lecture hall seat would allow. His knees bumped up against the wooden back of the pew before him, the thin wool of his trousers doing little to protect him from the hard surface. Wincing, he shifted. His elbow struck the fellow sitting next to him, the man shooting him a dark glare, his lips twisted in a moue of displeasure. Ignoring the throb of pain radiating from the offending limb, he offered a weak smile of apology. The man jerked his gaze back to the lecturer, muttering under his breath a litany of what was no doubt curses.

Surreptitiously rubbing his knee, he focussed his own attention on the lecturer. The man droned on, something about crosschecking corroborating evidence with the… Good God, but the man was boring. Stupidly, he'd thought the lecture series on the murder of a young London tailor apprentice a few years back would be of interest. As near as he could recollect, the case had been full of lurid and salacious details; however, the lecturer was turning what had been a scintillating case into something yawn-inducing. A dry delivery and an insistence on reciting verbatim the minutia of constable reports fairly guaranteed the boredom of all who'd attended.

Leaning back, he braced his elbow on the edge of the pew and amused himself with counting how many attendees were doodling in their notebooks.

Ten minutes later, the lecture hadn't become any more interesting, but there was something odd about the fellow before him. Arms now crossed, he examined the back of the fellow's head. Dark hair pulled back into an old-fashioned queue, adorned with a subdued black ribbon, shoulders slight, neck delicate, and if he didn't know better…

Bloody hell. He did know better.

Leaning forward, he arranged his arms on the back of her pew. "That's quite a convincing wig."

Etta stiffened.

A heady mix of amusement and exhilaration rushed through him. "Did you borrow clothes from your father?"

Her head whipped around. Gaze skewering him, she gritted out, "Be quiet."

The fellow next to him issued another dark look and pointedly moved three seats down.

It didn't deter him, however, and neither did her glare. "It's quite convincing, I vow. Most people wouldn't even notice."

"I'm trying to listen, and I don't want to be ejected." Her tone was forceful even as she strove for almost total silence, and then her glare faded into an expression that approached pleading. "*Please* be quiet."

That sobered him as nothing else could. He nodded, and, clearly relieved, she turned back to focus on the lecturer.

Abandoning the tedious lecturer, he instead studied her. It really was a good disguise. Strange she'd donned such an outfit to pass herself off as male. The Etta he knew would have bludgeoned her way into the lecture, seated herself, and refused to remove for God or anyone. This stealthy Etta was someone new.

A tiny portion of carrot-red hair had escaped the wig to curl around her neck. He fought the urge to tuck the hair beneath the wig and then run his fingers over the delicate skin. His hand would span her nape, his fingers reaching the wing of her shoulder blade. She'd tilt her head to the side, and he'd trace the cord the move revealed, fascinated by her reactions as her breath quickened and her skin heated. Her head would drop forward, and he'd lean over, wisps of red hair teasing his lips…

Clearing his throat, he shifted again in his seat and placed his hat over his lap.

As soon as the lecturer stepped from the lectern, Etta rose and darted toward the door. Shoving to his feet, Christopher followed her, weaving and dodging to keep the old-fashioned queue in sight.

Finally, in a quiet hallway, he caught up with her, rushing before her to block her exit. She tried to step around him, but he blocked that, too. Folding her arms, she set her stance, a rather magnificent scowl on her face.

Leaning against the wall, he crossed his arms as he gave her a lazy smile. "Do you often attend lectures dressed as a man?"

Shoulders sagging, she lost her scowl. Wrapping her arms about herself, she said, "I have tried to attend lectures as myself. It does not go well."

It hit him in the chest. Smile dissolving, he

uncrossed his arms. He wanted to go to her, to wrap her in his embrace and give her comfort. Etta Wilding-Marsh should never look so lost, so…defeated.

"I attended because I wish to start a new series." The words seemed as if someone else had spoken, though it was his voice.

Surprise lit her face, but surprise didn't come close to describing how he felt. He hadn't even admitted to himself he was going to attempt it. It was still diaphanous, forming in the ether and labelled with, *perhaps one day*.

"A new series?" Mouth twisting ruefully, she unlooped her arms from about herself. "A Gothic romance on criminal law. That has not been attempted before."

"No, not a Gothic." His palms were damp. Clearing his throat, he wiped his hands against his trousers. "I'm going to write something different. A detective novel. A series. Maybe a serial. I am not certain as yet, though I know it will feature a male detective and a gentlewoman with a penchant for solving crimes. But it will be a detective novel. A detective series. It will feature detectives." Bloody hell, he was babbling. He wiped his hands on his trousers again.

"A lady detective?" she finally asked.

"Yes. Well, no. I mean—" *Jesus wept, Hiddleston, get it together.* "That won't be her profession, but her inclination. He will be a private inquiry agent. Evans is a private inquiry agent and—" He stopped abruptly. "Do you recall him? Nathaniel Evans? He's one of the lads who attended The Havisham Arms with me."

She was quiet a moment. "Was he the surly

one?"

He nodded forcefully. "That's him. Surly, and impatient besides. But Evans—Nathaniel—he has said he will help with the research and ensuring the tone is correct and factual, not like the flim-flam I usually write—those were his words, by the way—and I thought today's lecture would help, but it ended up being extremely tedious, and then I saw you." He stopped, almost gasping for air. Goddamn, but he sounded like a madman.

"It was a tedious lecture, wasn't it?" Her fingers tapped at her side. "What is your novel to be about?"

A strange kind of excitement filled him. "I thought in the first novel, she could be a client of the inquiry agent and proves herself invaluable in solving the case. Of course, he thinks her frivolous to begin with, but, over the course of the novel, he realises she is more than what she seems and comes to rely upon her insight and counsel."

She regarded him for the longest time, so long his stomach felt like lead. "It sounds interesting," she finally said.

Relief tore through him, and he gave a cocky grin. "Of course it's interesting. I shall write it."

She rolled her eyes. "I should have known better than to think you would be serious for half a minute."

Sobering, he said, "Would you read it? If you saw it in a shop, would you pick it up?"

"Perhaps."

He released the breath he hadn't known he had taken. Her opinion mattered. It always had. In fact... "I should like it if you would consult on it."

She blinked. "I beg your pardon."

"I should like it if you would consult. Be my

editor, as it were." He warmed to the idea. "You were practically my editor on the first story anyway."

"I beg your pardon?"

"Your comments." She still looked utterly confused. "On the passages I included with the articles."

"You mean those Gothic scribbles you sent with the articles? You actually applied my criticisms?"

Now she seemed shocked as well as confused. "Of course. You were correct, every time." Here was a sight he'd never thought he'd see. Etta Wilding-Marsh, stymied. "Will you be my consultant?"

She seemed to snap herself out of it. "I shall have to think on it."

Something inside him dulled, but he swallowed it with a grin. "Don't think too long. Others would clamour for the opportunity."

"Then perhaps you should ask them."

He merely continued to grin.

"I have to go," she stammered. "Gwen—the duchess—is expecting me."

"Of course," he murmured.

She made to move past him only to hesitate. "You truly wish my opinion?"

"Of course."

A smile lit her face, blinding in its brilliance.

He sucked in his breath. Heart pounding, he nodded dumbly as she said another good-bye and left, glancing over her shoulder with another smile before disappearing around the corner.

Regaining his breath, he silently recounted the last few moments. He, apparently, was to write a series, and not just any series, but a detective series. Something he'd barely allowed himself to think of, he'd blurted out to Etta without a thought. And then, he'd asked her to help him with it. And she had smiled at him.

Slowly, he made his way from the lecture hall. He was supposed to call upon a Lady Gillmure and her reading group in an hour, part of the duchess's plan to drum up support for the school. He had to put thoughts of Etta Wilding-Marsh smiling behind him.

It was only... She had smiled at him.

Chapter Six

THE DINING TABLE WAS strewn with paper, empty teacups, and plates littered with crumbs. At the summit of the debris sat Gwen, muttering to herself as she scribbled furiously in a notepad. Flyaway strands of brown hair haloed her head and a faint streak of ink blemished one cheek. She also had three pencils adorning her upswept hair.

Head propped in her hand, Etta took a breath and refocussed on the page before her. They'd been in the dining room for most of the day, dealing with the business of organisation. They had a fete to organise, and another reading, and they had yet to determine the exact parameters of the scholarship. So much work lay before them as to be insurmountable, but she'd never let the impossible fell her before.

Exhaling, she allowed herself some relief, cradling her head in her hands. A pain had lodged itself below her left shoulder blade and her lower back was tight and tense.

The door opened. The Duke of Sowrith entered the room, the drag of his left leg almost imperceptible. Gwen didn't look up from her work, clearly absorbed the papers before her.

The duke made his way to his wife, placing his hand gently on her shoulder. Blinking, she glanced up and, upon spying her husband, the most intensely joyful smile lit her face. "Edward."

The duke returned her smile, the scar pulling at the left side of his mouth. "Busy?"

Her friend's brow puckered. "Yes, dash it all. This is fair to drive me insane. What made me think this was a good idea?"

Brushing a kiss against her hair, he then proceeded to remove the pencils. "Because it is a good idea." He held them out to her.

Absently, she took them. "Yes, I suppose."

The duke's gaze drifted over debris on the table. "Have you eaten?"

Gwen waved at the discarded plates. "Yes."

The duke's expression turned to resignation. "That is not food, Gwen."

"Scones are food," she argued.

"Have you had a break? Rested? You seem harried."

"There's so much to do."

"That's no excuse for no rest."

"But—"

"You will rest, Duchess," he said formally. His gaze flicked to Etta. "You, too, Miss Wilding-Marsh."

She had been remembered. Wasn't that nice? She nodded, resisting the urge to fold her arms tightly about herself.

Gwen glanced down at the papers before her. "I'll just finish this last seating chart—"

"You will not." The duke hauled his wife to her feet. "You will come with me, and you will rest."

"But Edward—"

"You won't do anyone any good if you wear away to nothing."

Grumbling, she allowed him to usher her from the room.

Left alone with a mound of paper, Etta succumbed to her urge and wrapped her arms about herself. Gaze wandering around the room, she rubbed her upper arms. There was nothing familiar here, nothing of comfort. She was alone, again, and there was no one to care if she were rested and well—

Abruptly, she stood. Arms still wrapped about herself, she exited the room to stride down a hallway blindly. She did not know what she sought, only that she needed to be away from the dining room, needed to find something of comfort, something to make her think of things other than the expression on the duke's face as he pushed Gwen's hair behind her ear.

A faint glow of candlelight from beneath a door drew her. She pushed it open, only to halt mid-step.

Sprawled in a chair on the far side of the library, in a state of advanced dishabille, was Lord Christopher Hiddleston. Eyes closed, head resting against the back of the chair, he seemed tired, his long legs spread carelessly before him.

Hesitant, she wavered on the threshold.

"You'll let in a draft," he said without opening his eyes.

She started. "Beg pardon?"

"Don't hover. You're letting the warmth out."

"My apologies," she said tartly. Hesitation held her again. "I should not enter. You are not dressed."

Cracking an eye, he glanced down at himself. "Everything's covered."

It was and yet it…wasn't. That must be the

cause of her hesitation. The impropriety of it all. She ignored the voice that said it had never bothered her before. "You are not wearing a jacket, your waistcoat is unbuttoned, and your shirt is untied."

Eyes again closed, he shrugged. "In or out. Decide."

She bit her lip. "I should go."

Exhaling, he pinched the bridge of his nose. "Why?"

"Don't you want to relax?"

"I am relaxing." He remained sprawled in the chair, eyes closed, and arms draped over the armrests. Dark flesh painted half-circles beneath his eyes while a reddish beard stubbled his strong jaw. Deep lines bracketed his mouth, and a pucker had formed between his brows, one she found for some insane reason she wanted to soothe.

Slowly, she made her way into the library and sank into a chair. Running her gaze over him, she studied his tired frame. He wanted her opinion. This man, who had made himself the bane of her existence, who had refused to leave her in peace for a decade, wished for her counsel on his novels and she…she couldn't decide. She went one way, and then another, and, above all, she couldn't think *why*. Why did he want her opinion? Why did it matter? And why did the thought of him desiring her opinion make her…happy.'

Her brows drew. Happy? It wasn't quite that emotion, but something similar. Something warm and exhilarating and… She didn't know.

Looking at him now, resting exhausted in a chair, that same feeling rushed over her, threaded with concern and a desire to care for him, to make it so the exhaustion left his features, and he again turned that wicked grin upon her. "I will work with you."

He opened one eye.

She lifted her chin. Uncertainty made her falter, and she despised faltering. "I will work with you. On your lady detective."

Both eyes snapped open. "You will?"

She nodded. "Yes."

The most glorious smile lit his face.

Quickly, she averted her gaze. *You have no call to think his smile glorious, Etta Wilding-Marsh. Get your mind back where it belongs.* Crossing her arms, she affected a glare. "It had better not be claptrap."

"It won't." He straightened in the chair, the tiredness falling away. "It will be the very best I can make it. And it will be even better with you to ensure I don't fall to lazy habits."

He truly did esteem her opinion. He spoke and his lips formed words, the upper thin and well-defined, the points forming a sharp bow. His lower lip was full, generous and...and she shouldn't be thinking of his lips.

"Don't you think?"

She snapped back to attention. "I apologise, my mind was elsewhere."

His face fell, but quickly he recovered, that infernal grin taking residence. "The trope is tired, but it's what the public demand. I've seen it time and again and—"

She placed her hand on his.

Abruptly silent, his gaze whipped to hers then fell to where her hand covered his. Belatedly, she realised he wore no gloves and neither did she. She could feel the strength in his hand, the warmth. His fingers were long and well-formed, the nails short and neat. Breath caught in her throat, she controlled the urge to flex her fingers to trace the veins in the back of his hand. To feel more of his strength, his warmth.

She cleared her throat. "I apologise. I allowed my thoughts to wander, which is inexcusable."

Dramatically, he laid his hand over his heart. "You did not listen to my every word? I am devastated. Completely ruined. Desolate and ravaged."

"I'm glad you know how to use a thesaurus," she said sourly.

He grinned.

"Have you written anything as yet?"

"Scraps only. Not enough to show you, but I will have something for you before the week is out."

So quick? "There's no need to rush."

"I want to." He grinned again, and this time it was an inclusive one, inviting her to share his enthusiasm. "I want you to see what I'm capable of."

Nonplussed, she settled into her chair as he launched again into a description of his plans. This was all so very odd. He seemed to hold her opinion in high regard, but how was it he, of all people, would do so? She had, time and again, been urged to silence, to keep quiet her thoughts and opinions. Even Gwen had occasionally said such. She had learnt early that if she did not speak, none would ask.

Something warm settled beneath her breast, small and undefined but glowing with every word he spoke. And now here was Christopher, the boy who had been the bane of her existence. Asking.

The world had turned upside down, and she needed to make sense of it. But first, she would listen to him, allow herself the pleasure his condescension caused, and she would not question or second guess.

Well. She would try.

Chapter Seven

CLARISSA FAIRWEATHER HAD THE advantage, a determined expression setting her features as she lined up her mallet and ball. The croquet match had turned vicious in the last few minutes, Lucy Marcham realising she was getting an absolute pounding and stepping up her game.

Holding a glass of lemonade, Etta watched from the edge of the green, shielded from the view of most by two willow trees. Almost as soon as she'd arrived at the fete she'd stationed herself here, far from the mill of the crowd, and it was only now the croquet game had commenced that others began to encroach upon her solitude. Judging by the turnout, the fete could be counted a wild success, even if it was in support of a school most in attendance thought scandalous...and not in a good way. However, the draw of a new duchess, a duke who rarely appeared in society, and a handful of the most notorious Gothic and adventure novelists in England brought Cambridge society in droves.''

A commotion near the tent drew her attention. A gaggle of people—from the way they squawked she could not refer to them as anything other—approached, clustered around a central person. Dark-auburn hair appeared briefly, along with a wicked grin, and then his eyes met hers and the grin turned genuine. Warm. Almost as if he were glad to see her.

Her heart tripped in her chest.

Staring out into the distance, she took a calming breath. This was ridiculous. She shouldn't be feeling such about *him*. It didn't matter if he thought her clever, or sweet, or anything. It didn't matter that his face lit when he saw her, that he looked as if he would push through those clamouring for his attention to be by her side. There could be no truth in such a look, and she abhorred liars.

"Why are you hiding over here?" Skin pale, eyes dark, Gwen came to a halt next to her, rubbing her forearm as her gaze darted from the fete to the house and back again.

"I'm not hiding. I'm in full view of the fete." She hadn't even seen her friend approach. Damnation, when would this blasted fascination with the man stop? "Besides, I'm cheering Clarissa Fairweather. She's thrashing Lucy Marcham."

Gwen's teeth worried her lip. "You should enjoy the fete, Etta."

"I am. I'm drinking lemonade." She held up her glass.

Her friend barely spared it a glance. "Surely you can spare a moment or two to rub a few shoulders. Be sociable, laugh at their stories, that sort of thing."

"Me?" Now it was her turn for disbelief. Had Gwen forgotten what it was like? Always there was distance between them and society. At each gathering, it would be Gwen and her against the world. But now it was only her, and the world never let her forget she was against them.

Gwen wrapped her arms about herself. "I can't do it on my own."

"I can't do it at all." Etta gestured with her glass. "They don't like me. They never have."

"Only because you dismiss them. Why can't you be agreeable, even if you don't mean it?"

A kernel of hurt burned in her chest, but she pushed it aside. "What, exactly, are you suggesting?"

"Walk amongst them, smile, and listen. I know it's a lot to ask, but I can't do it by myself."

"I am not the one who wanted this fete, Gwen."

"No, but it's the only way. We must obtain funds somehow, and these people are the way to do it. Do you think I like parading myself before them? Do you think I enjoy subjecting Edward to their scrutiny? He hates people staring at him, and yet he endures it because he knows what this school means to me. Is it too much to ask that you are pleasant for five minutes at a time?"

"I never claimed to be sociable, and my talents do not lie in that direction. I came to this fete to support the school."

"As well you should, the school was your idea."

"It may have been my idea, but you are the one who is compromising. These people couldn't care less about a female law school, and yet here they are to gawk and stare. We should not suffer their condescension."

"And yet this is how things get done!" Gwen's voice rang through the field. Some at the far refreshment table turned to regard them in surprise. "You only ever see black and white," she continued in a lowered voice as the guests turned back to their own conversations, eyes burning. "But the world doesn't work like that. Not even the *law* works like that."

Clenching her fists at her sides, Etta set her jaw. "Maybe I should just go home, then."

"Maybe you should."

"Fine."

"Fine."

For a moment, they stared at each other and then, in unison, they turned on their heels to storm in opposite directions.

Etta stalked deeper into the trees surrounding the field. Chest heaving, she stopped under a willow, and, before she could take another step, great sobs overwhelmed her.

Slumping against the trunk, she buried her face in her hands. She didn't even know why she and Gwen had argued. She knew she should socialise, should tone down her opinions, but it was how she *was*. She couldn't change her nature, but it seemed everyone wanted her to.

Wiping at her cheeks, she set her jaw. Maybe she was in the wrong. Maybe it was she should circulate the crowd. Maybe she should swallow her comments and her ire and attempt conversation and...

"What are you doing over here?"

She whipped around. Christopher—Lord Christopher—stood there, that same smile on his face, the one that said he was glad to see her.

Liar.

Lifting her chin, she gave him a look she knew to be belligerent and dismissive at once. "I don't see what concern it is of yours."

Smile fading, he searched her face. "Are you well?"

She wiped impatiently at her face. "I'm fine."

"Are you certain? You don't appear yourself."

"I am perfectly well. Shouldn't you be out there, amongst your public?"

"Probably, but I'd rather be here with you."

Well, he was in the minority. "Was there something you wanted?"

"As a matter of fact, I did."

She waited.

Brows drawn, he studied her.

Lifting her chin, she said, "Well?"

Seeming to make some decision, he grinned. "I have pages."

"Pages?"

He produced a notebook and handed it to her. "Pages."

The book contained page after page of tightly spaced writing, diagrams and lines that looped over themselves. "What is this?"

"It's my detective novel. Or the bones of it, in any event."

Something in his tone made her glance up. Concern painted his features, but his brow quickly smoothed and his usual smirk took residence. No, it wasn't really a smirk. It was more a grin. Or maybe just amusement.

She shook herself. Lord, who cared what to term his expression? In any event, this was distraction, and she welcomed it.

She thumbed through the pages. The bones of a story were there, and the introduction of the characters. They fairly leapt off the page, the staid inquiry agent Edmund Ballantine and the vivacious Lady Penelope. "You wrote all of this in three days?"

"I would have written more, but I had

commitments." He looked about them. "I'm going to sit," he announced, and then he virtually collapsed onto the ground, his long legs sprawled before him.

Lowering herself with substantially more decorum, she arranged her skirts in precise folds, laying the pages atop her lap. This was truly amazing. How did he do it? How did he write so fast?

"What do you think?" he asked, leaning back on his hands.

"I think it's good." His thigh was near hers, so close they almost touched. Concentrating on the pages in her hands, she stared until the ink began to run together.

"So, what in particular?"

"You've only just given it to me. Perhaps if I'd had more than a cursory glance, I might be able to give an informed critique."

He snorted. "An informed critique? Why on earth would one desire such a thing? No, a half-baked, ill-conceived bare whiff of a notion will suffice."

She battled the twitch of her lips. She would not reward such nonsense. She absolutely refused. "Why do you write?"

Clearly surprised by her sudden question, he answered, "Because I like it." He looked ridiculously comfortable, sprawled as he was. "Because I have to."

The fabric of his grey trousers outlined the heavy muscles in his long legs. A queer feeling began in her belly and her breasts.

Dragging her eyes from him, she told herself the sight of him made her feel nothing at all. Or, if it did, it was purely annoyance. Yes, that's what it was. Definitely. "What do you mean?"

"I don't know. I just must. It's what I've always done." He tilted his head back. "Well, you know. I always had a book with me.

His throat held for her a strange fascination. The lightest of stubble caught the sun, shining a red kind of gold. "Yes, but I didn't know you were obsessed."

"Of course you did. You used to jape me about it all the time."

"What? When?" As soon as she said it, she remembered. He always had one book or another with him, and they were always sensational in nature, invariably from the Minerva Press or some other disreputable publisher. "Why did you read them?"

He shrugged. "I liked them."

Apparently, that was reason enough. She opened her mouth to argue, only to pause. Why should there be a more involved reason? Because he liked it was perfectly valid. "I'm sorry."

His brow puckered. "For what?"

"For making fun."

How was it he could stagger while seated? "It cannot be true. Henrietta Wilding-Marsh apologising to me?"

She scowled. "I'll take it back."

Clearly knowing her words for the empty threat they were, he smiled winsomely, auburn hair a tumble over his brow, his throat strong, his shoulders broad and shown to advantage by his dark jacket.

That queer feeling began again in her stomach. Glancing away, she cursed her weak nature. How was it she was swayed by a pretty face? Further, she had a horrible feeling she was only swayed by *his* pretty face.

"Come now, I must show you a particular

passage." Placing his hand behind her, he leaned over her to thumb the pages with the other. "I found myself inspired, by no more than it was two o'clock in the morning and I'd just consumed a particularly fine cup of chocolate."

He hadn't noticed she'd frozen. Warm breath stirred the strands of her hair, while his fingers bumped hers as he turned the page. Determinedly, she focussed on the notebook. She would not notice the brush of his arm against her, the firmness of the muscle beneath his coat and shirt. She wouldn't.

"Etta?"

Swallowing, she turned her head. Her gaze fell upon his lips, so near her own.

His tongue darted out to wet them. As if it were someone else, she saw her hand lift to capture a lock of his hair. The fiery strands were cool to her touch, and soft. The curl wound about her finger, as if it wouldn't let go.

"Etta?" he asked again, his voice husky.

Cold reality slapped her. Horrified, she launched to her feet, stumbling a little.

He struggled to a half-sitting, half-standing position, hovering awkwardly. "Etta—"

"I must— I will—" She couldn't form a coherent thought. Abandoning the attempt, she fled.

Mind a whirl, she dashed across the field. First the fight with Gwen and then the…the…whatever that was with Christoph—with *Lord Christopher*.

The crinkle of paper in her hand drew her attention. His pages. She still had his pages.

Slowing to a measured pace, she glanced toward the fete. She needed distraction. She needed to occupy her mind so she wouldn't think of the disaster this day had become. She would socialise. She would be personable even if it killed her, and if Maria Seebolm or Octavia Fairchild saw fit to snark, she would grit her teeth, smile, and take it in her stride.

It didn't matter that Gwen was mad at her, and she wouldn't think about Christopher at all.

Chapter Eight

EYES DOWNCAST, ETTA PUSHED a pea around her plate. A lock of red hair flirted with her bent neck, tempting Christopher to smooth it back into place and replace its gentle caress with his own. Or, better yet, he would trace its path with his lips, savouring the gasp she would try to disguise as he followed the cord of her neck down to the hollow of her throat. Stealthily, he'd trace his hand up her to cover her breast. She'd shiver and stifle a moan, her hands clenched into fists even as she leaned into his caress. She'd fight herself—because when did Etta not fight?—but in the end, her feelings would overwhelm her and she'd spear her fingers into his hair, haul his mouth to hers, and—

"Don't you agree, Hiddleston?"

With a start, he tore his gaze from Etta to focus on her father. Neck hot, he resisted the urge to adjust his collar. "I beg your pardon, sir?"

Professor Wilding-Marsh exhaled impatiently. "Patent law, Hiddleston, and its growing importance in this new age. I've been speaking of it for the last five minutes."

"Right, sir. Apologies, sir." Christ, the professor made him feel again like a green student, newly arrived at Cambridge and still wet behind the ears. He'd taken Professor Wilding-Marsh's lectures, along with his mates Evans, Cartwright, and Davenport. The man had installed the fear of God into his students with his steely glare and cutting words, making it so one knew when the professor was disappointed, and he'd been disappointed often.

Plus, it didn't help he was having completely inappropriate thoughts regarding the man's daughter. "I am not familiar with patent law, sir. I focussed on other disciplines."

Professor Wilding-Marsh merely grunted.

Etta hadn't responded to his remonstration, instead watching as a pea dribbled off the blade of her knife to drown in a puddle of gravy. She'd said little and eaten less, glancing often at the dining room door as if she wished to be anywhere but here. He hadn't seen her since the fete three days prior. She hadn't visited Bennet Close or the duchess, and she'd attended none of the events he'd frequented. He'd even gone back to the Havisham Arms of an evening, hoping she would be there. She hadn't.

Besides the fact he simply wished to see her, she had his pages. He'd written more, but he needed those pages to make certain the story made sense. At the very least, she could make herself available after agreeing to work with him on Lady Penelope and Edmund Ballantine.

The professor exhaled forcefully. "Henrietta, say something. I can't be carrying the conversation."

She pushed a pea around her plate.

"Henrietta!"

Dark-brown eyes met Christopher's. He felt it

like a punch to the gut, that dark, intense gaze, the intelligence burning within, the passion.

Her gaze slid to her father. "And of what am I to speak?"

The professor scowled. "You are the female, and thus the hostess. You should know how to carry a conversation."

Jaw set, she turned to Christopher. "My lord, what subjects do you believe should first be taught at Sowrith College once it opens?"

"Henrietta," the professor said in warning.

She ignored him. "Lord Christopher?"

Before he could speak, the professor interjected. "Hiddleston, I apologise. My daughter is on another of her tirades and speaks of things of which she knows little."

Etta abandoned her knife with a clatter. "Sowrith College can only be of benefit. Surely even you can see that."

"You don't know what you speak of, girl. Leave this to those with the greater knowledge."

"And who has greater knowledge? Tell me, Father, whose opinion should I seek?"

The professor's breath exploded. "Don't be facetious, girl. It doesn't change the fact a female school is a ridiculous notion, and Sowrith should take his duchess in hand before she embarrasses him entirely. What woman possesses the wherewithal, the *intellect*, to learn, and most especially, to learn the law? It is distinctly unfeminine and a purely masculine pursuit."

"A masculine pursuit? And yet, even now, there are numerous schools devoted to the education of young women."

"Furthering their talents in the gentle arts, those

that are pleasing in females and help prepare her for matrimony and motherhood."

"Not only that. There is the study of philosophy, of art, of music and economy." Chest heaving, eyes blazing, she skewered her father with her gaze. "Women are capable of more than you can imagine, and many seek to better their circumstances. Many strive for a better life, a *richer* life, and who are you to stand in their way?"

"For the love of God, Henrietta, there is no need to become emotional." The professor glanced at Christopher askance and rolled his eyes.

Folding his arms, he maintained a blank expression. He would not be counted in solidarity with this man.

"Emotion has nothing to do with it," Etta said. "Why shouldn't women be allowed to study law? My sex is just as capable as men of logic and reason, and logic states one half of the population should be allowed to—"

"Henrietta. Enough. You are speaking again on subjects which you do not understand. I do not know how God saw fit to give me such a daughter. This is your mother's fault, abandoning her family and her place."

"But Father—"

"No, Henrietta." The professor's tone was final.

She slumped into her chair, her eyes trained once more on her plate.

"Smile, Henrietta," the professor said. "No one likes a sour female."

Christopher couldn't take his eyes from Etta. He'd never seen her dejected before. A burn started in his chest, a mix of pain and anger.

Throwing his napkin to the table, the professor

rose. "Well, that's dinner done. I am off to the chambers. Hiddleston, a pleasure."

Was he seriously going to depart, flouting all rules of polite society and leave his unmarried daughter alone with a man to whom she was not related? "Yes. A pleasure."

The professor strode from the room without a backward glance.

It seemed, indeed, he would.

Etta was slumped in her chair, one arm wrapped around her stomach as she rubbed at something on the tablecloth.

Closing his mouth, he turned to her. "Did your father just leave?"

She sat up straight. "Yes. Would you like dessert?"

"Your father just left. The house."

"Yes."

"Leaving you with a man to whom you are not related."

"This is not a troublesome thing."

"Yes, it is," he exploded. "It is a troublesome thing. *I* am troubled. Is this the care he takes of you? Is this how he shows his concern?"

Her brow creased. "It is how he's always been, but I am not often home for dinner. The Havisham does well, or when Gwen is home, I—" She paled. Swallowing, she continued, "I do not often eat here."

"How he's—" Of a sudden, her presence at The Havisham Arms all those years ago made sense. How it was always she and Gwen alone, never accompanied. Never protected. "My god." Rubbing his jaw, he shook his head. "My god."

Brows drawn and clearly confused, she said, "Are you well?"

He wanted to go to her. He wanted wrap her in his embrace and never let her go. Did her father not know the lively, passionate, intelligent woman his daughter was?

Exhaling, he placed his hands on the table. "How can he treat you such? Those things he said... He discounts your opinion as if it is nothing. Does he not know his daughter? Does he not know the amazing brain you have? My god, I had to work to keep up with you. Every argument you countered, with passion and vigour. He is a fool if he does not see it. If he doesn't see *you*."

Etta stared at him and the next thing he knew, she'd somehow made her way around the table, her arms were about him, and her lips were on his.

Before he could react, she pulled back, her expression falling. "Did I not do it right?"

Why did she think that, because he hadn't immediately responded? How could he, when she'd taken him completely by surprise? "Etta—"

She continued as if he hadn't spoken. "I knew I wouldn't do it right, I knew it would be disaster and...oh Lord, it was a disaster, wasn't it? Why did I even attempt it? I apologise, I apologise profusely—"

"Etta."

She fell silent, wide brown eyes drowning him.

Cupping her face, he said, "I'm going to kiss you now."

"Oh." She closed her eyes. "All right."

He brushed his lips against hers, soft, tentative. She made a small noise, not quite a sigh, and he pulled back. She followed, seeking him, soft lips slightly parted and he took advantage, pushing inside. Her chest hitched against his, and then she melted.

Holding her head steady, he tangled his fingers

in her hair. The carrot-coloured strands slipped through his fingers, cool against his skin. He kissed her until his jaw ached and his heart pounded, and he wanted more, he wanted all of her, always.

But this was not the time nor the place. Pulling back, he pressed light kisses to her brow, her cheek, and wrestled himself back to control. Eyes closed, she sighed, her hands stroking his back. Emotion flooded him, so big he couldn't contain it. He'd never felt this with another woman, but this wasn't any woman. This was Etta.

She placed her head on his chest. Looping his arms about her, he felt…contentment. "Have you commented on my pages?"

A few moments of silence, and then: "Oh. Your book."

"Yes. My book." A smile tugged at his lips. "Have you?"

"Not as yet. I've been busy."

"Busy? With what?"

"Oh, you know. Things."

"The school?"

"Yes. The school."

Why did he feel that was not the truth? Pulling back, he studied her. She was pale, and a lingering unhappiness haunted her eyes. "Is all well?"

She exhaled impatiently. "Of course it is. Just because I have not had the time to look at your manuscript does not mean something is ill. I am busy. That is all."

The corner of his lip twitched. She got her back up so easily, but some of the sadness had faded with the rise of her ire.

Another comfortable silence.

"Gwen's mad at me."

Surprise had him pulling back. "Pardon?"

Lifting her head from his chest, miserable brown eyes met his. "Gwen. She's angry with me."

"Why?"

"I don't know. She said it was because I wasn't socialising at the fete, but she knows what I'm like. I am not...sociable." She took a breath. "You know, I never see her. Not anymore." Her voice was small. "She's my family, and I never... She lives in Devon now. She's so far away. And I know she works so hard. She's working so hard to make the school a reality, and I know the duke is not comfortable in society that is not hers."

He didn't know what to say, how to make it better. He could only listen and hope that helped.

"I know all this. I know it, but it doesn't... She won't..." She closed her eyes, swallowed. "Do you think she still likes me?"

Christ. Etta. Cupping her cheek, he urged her to look at him. She did, her eyes wet with unshed tears. "Of course she does. You had a difference of opinion. You will apologise, or she will, and all will be as it was before."

She bit her lip. "Are you certain?"

"As certain as I am of anything." He stroked her hair.

"I'm to dine at Bennett Close tomorrow night." She hesitated. "Will you be there?"

"Yes." He would make it so he was there, beside her.

A shuddering sigh and then the tiniest of smiles before she nestled against him once more.

Tightening his arms about her, he stared at the wall. How was it Etta Wilding-Marsh had come to mean so much to him? He wanted to make everything

better for her, wanted to make it so she never felt
pain. He couldn't shield her from hurt, but he could
offer his comfort and hope it helped.

And tomorrow, when she dined at Bennett
Close, he would be there to help in any way he could.

Chapter Nine

WINE GLASS RAISED TO her lips, Etta watched Christopher across the expanse of the dining table. Hair aflame in the candlelight, the shadows licked his cheekbones and caressed the cord of his neck. His gloved hand lay careless across his place setting, the fine white cloth stretched tight over his knuckles, the breadth of his hand…and that's when she realised she was staring at Christopher Hiddleston's hand.

She took a sip of wine. He and the duke conversed, discussing some Gothic novel she'd never heard of. The evening had been torturous. No wonder she chose to stare at Christopher rather than face the fact that Gwen could barely look at her. Upon her arrival, Gwen had sat with her eyes lowered and her hands in her lap, and the duke had carried the conversation. The duke, it should be noted, did not wear the mantle of host well. The ensuring half hour had been one of the most awkward she'd ever endured, and not even the arrival of Christopher had alleviated it.

Christopher, to his credit, had taken on the

duties of host, skilfully leading the conversation to mundane topics such as the weather and what entertainments would be held at the next ball. She'd snuck a glance at Gwen every half a moment or so, but she'd never caught her friend's eye. Her former friend? Oh lord, she hoped not her former friend.

Chest tight, she placed her glass carefully on the table before her. She hadn't had so much to drink to warrant such care, or at least she thought she hadn't, but she couldn't count on steady hands. She would think on other things, things that didn't involve her oldest friendship or how it might be over. She would think instead of Christopher.

Why did she find him so fascinating? She'd merely glance at him, and then she'd find herself lost in contemplation of the cut of his cheekbones or the length of his lashes. Heat would swirl low in her belly, and she'd be overwhelmed with the urge to measure the length of his jaw with kisses…and then with her tongue.

Damnation, she was staring at him again. Taking another sip of wine, she forced herself to contemplate something other than him.

"How is your school, my dear?"

The duke's voice sliced through the room. Etta's gaze slid to Gwen. Her friend—was she still her friend?—looked grim. "We've received tacit approval from the building commission to erect a structure."

"Have you? And what else?" The duke's words sounded overly bright. She could not remember ever hearing such a tone from him before.

"Tomorrow, we're meeting with the building committee to start the ball rolling. It's quite possible we could break ground before the year is out." No enthusiasm lit Gwen's voice, her face without expression.

The duke wore his half-smile, the one that didn't pull at his scar, but it seemed tonight to wear a veil of desperation. "That's outstanding. You've done such good work. I can't believe you've organised all of this in less than a year. With, of course, Miss Wilding-Marsh." The duke's one-eyed gaze flicked to Etta.

Colour rode high on Gwen's cheeks. "Yes. Etta can often direct people to behave as she wishes."

Fingers curling in her lap, she glanced down at her plate. "It wasn't hard."

"It never is," Gwen muttered.

"Miss Wilding-Marsh often persuades those to courses other than they intended." Christopher's smile had an edge to it, a kind of flirtation.

Grateful for the distraction, she raised a brow. "I seem to remember many occasions where you were determined to hold an opinion clearly incorrect."

"And you always insisted, loudly, on my correction."

She grinned for half a moment before her gaze again rested upon Gwen. All humour and warmth fled.

A hush fell on the table. Awkward silence rose, the clink of cutlery and crystal abnormally loud.

Finally, Gwen stood. "We should leave the gentlemen to their devices."

Etta rose slowly. She didn't want to be alone with Gwen. She didn't want the opportunity to discover if Gwen still considered her a friend.

Christopher caught her eye. The corner of his mouth lifted, and in that small expression she read his comfort and his encouragement. So buoyed, she straightened and followed Gwen from the room.

The drawing room was one she'd been in dozens of times over the past fortnight. Uncertain what she should do, she hovered in the door as Gwen seated herself on the chaise. Should she sit opposite as she'd done earlier in the week? But that was before their argument. Should she launch into conversation, perhaps about the school, as she had four days ago? But again, that was before.

The silence was deafening.

Their gazes met.

Etta had no idea what to do with her hands, and Gwen appeared just as ill-at-ease, her grey eyes miserable. Hesitantly, she took a step toward Gwen, and Gwen took one as well, and suddenly they were before each other, gripping each other's hands tight.

"I'm sorry," they both said, and then both started speaking at once.

"I'm truly sorry. I had no right—"

"*I* had no right." Gwen's hands tightened on Etta's. "I shouldn't have snapped at you, even with Edward and the planning and my work…"

"No, I understand. I should have done more, shouldered more of the burden."

"You are already doing so much—

"But not enough. I shouldn't have left everything to you."

"You *haven't* left everything to me." Gwen tugged at her hands. "You haven't, Etta. You've done so much, and I'm a horrible, ungrateful cow to suggest otherwise."

Incredibly, a smile tugged at her. "A cow?"

Gwen nodded. "A horrible one."

Slowly, her smile faded. "I should have been more understanding."

"As should I." Gwen's breath shuddered. "But we could spend all night talking of who is more to blame when, instead, you could be telling me everything that has happened these last few days."

Horribly, heat burned her cheeks.

Her friend's eyes widened. "Henrietta Wilding-Marsh, what have you been up to?"

"Nothing," she mumbled.

"It is not nothing. Clearly it is *something*." Gwen tugged her to the chaise. "Tell me everything."

Reluctantly, she allowed herself to be led, sinking to the chaise as she madly tried to think of something to tell Gwen. Besides the truth.

"Don't even think of trying to tell me a story. You're a horrible liar."

"I am not."

"You are. And don't think I don't know what you're doing. You won't distract me."

Succumbing to the inevitable, she said, "I've been— I have started— Christopher and I—"

Gwen's eyes widened. "Christopher?"

She couldn't answer, had no idea how to answer.

"Is Lord Christopher Hiddleston *courting* you?"

She managed a sharp nod.

Gwen's face exploded in a grin. "I knew it! I told Edward, I said 'Lord Christopher has always singled Etta out, I would not be surprised if he sought to deepen their connection,' but I didn't know if you'd be amenable and now I find you are! Oh, this is amazing!"

"No, it's not. It's strange, and disturbing, and I've disliked him for so long. How can I allow him to court me?" She didn't understand how he could go from being the bane of her existence, someone who she could happily never see again, to being the person she wanted to share everything with, such that her day was incomplete if she didn't see him.

"Does there have to be a reason, Etta? Can't it simply be because you have discovered you like him?"

Uncertainty filled her. She'd forced these thoughts aside, had refused to dwell on these questions. Now, she had to think about these things, and she found she had no answers.

Gwen smiled brightly. "I received a new packet from Beecham Chambers yesterday and I've yet to look at it. I feel certain there are deed proposals relating to land surrounding Sowrithil and you know I dislike interpreting that language."

Grateful for the change in subject, she returned her friend's smile. "That is because you enjoy the sensational rather than the pragmatic."

"Sadly, tragically, that is the truth. It is a burden I must bear." She sighed dramatically.

Etta laughed and settled in for a lively discussion on the merits of land ownership.

***

CHECKING HER REFLECTION, ETTA made a face at the usual disaster of her hair and smoothed her gown. Exiting the chamber, she made her way toward the parlour, a lightness in her step. It felt wonderful to have made peace with Gwen, to know her friend didn't despise her and was awaiting her return to the drawing room, the duke and Christopher not yet having joined them.

Turning a corner, she squeaked as strong arms grabbed her and drew her into a darkened alcove. The squeak turned to a moan as Christopher's mouth covered hers. Wrapping her arms about him, she pulled him close as his thigh nudged her legs apart, every inch of his body against every inch of hers. Pleasure ran through her, and she wanted him closer, as close as he could be.

He coaxed her lips open, and his taste rushed through her.

He pulled back, resting his forehead against hers. "I've been wanting to do that all evening."

Tightening her hands in the fabric of his jacket, she struggled to regain her breath.

"Etta," he said softly, his hand stroking her hair.

"Yes?" she managed, finally able to let loose the fabric and feel instead him.

"Nothing. Just Etta." His lips feathered over her temple. "I missed you."

She smiled. "It's not even been an hour."

"I know." His arms tightened about her.

Closing her eyes, she rested her head on his shoulder, and, for one brief moment, she allowed herself to believe his charming lie. "I should get to the parlour."

"And I return to the dining room."

Neither of them moved.

"Gwen's forgiven me."

The corner of his mouth lifted. "I told you."

"You did."

He clutched his chest. "Do not tell me Etta Wilding-Marsh has *agreed* with me?"

She nuzzled his chin. "She has."

Finally, she forced herself from his arms. She got two steps before he pulled her back. He kissed the smile on her lips before she firmed her resolve and pushed from him, making her way down the hall.

She couldn't rid herself of her grin. Maybe Gwen was right. Maybe it didn't matter why she liked him, only that she did.

Maybe it didn't even matter that she thought she might be falling in love with him.

Chapter Ten

ACROSS THE BALLROOM, CHRISTOPHER was holding court, deftly conversing with a clutch of admirers, each one hanging on his every word.

Etta smiled as he smiled, the wide grin he called his 'professional welcoming author smile.' He'd explained he wanted his readers to feel included, and he never wanted them to feel he didn't appreciate them. She had asked what made it different from any other smile, and he'd proceeded to demonstrate, punctuating each with a corresponding kiss. A bubble of remembered warmth rose in her chest and she ghosted her fingers over her brow, her cheek, her jaw.

For a week now, they had been together most days, often dining with Gwen and the duke. She couldn't believe how happy she felt. She had her closest friend, and she had a man who made her feel glorious, whose smile and attention were more than she'd ever expected. She had never before been the focus of a person's attention, had never before felt she was necessary to them. Christopher made her feel that, that she alone was special to him.

They'd spoken of the years they'd been apart, and the years before when they'd argued in The Havisham Arms. He said he'd always liked her, that he spoke such because he knew if she was arguing with him then he was present to her, and, of course, he liked the sight of her in a temper. As he'd said this with a grin, she knew he was stirring. He said he'd been a blockhead to garner her attention, that he desired it above all things, and he disliked she so easily dismissed him. He'd made a face and said how much of a fool did that make him, and she'd thrown her arms about him and whispered she was glad he hadn't given up, that he'd sent her those articles, that he'd made her *see* him. His arms had tightened about her and he'd whispered back he was glad he was a fool, that he had her now and he would never let her go…

Someone jostled her elbow, reminding her she attended a ball with a veritable host of other people. With a scowl, Etta rounded upon them, ready to lambast, but they'd passed without even glancing her way, engrossed in their own conversation.

Ire thwarted, she crossed her arms and her gaze, as ever, drifted again to Christopher. He had a new gaggle, these even more enthralled than the last.

"Do you think he has a sweetheart?"

The rich tones of Olivia Thriby-Waite cut through Etta's thoughts.

"Lord Christopher? Of course he does. He's the handsomest man here. He would have at least a dozen." Roberta Crawford. She and Olivia Thriby-Waite stood behind her, clearly unconcerned with who might be listening.

"A dozen, Roberta? Surely not so many."

"Enough that we should not have a chance, no

matter our wealth or our beauty."

Etta tried to tune them out, but she couldn't stop herself from listening. They were talking of *Christopher*.

"Besides," Roberta Crawford continued. "He is from London. Do you believe he will stay in Cambridge, when there are the delights of Town society to draw him home?"

Olivia Thriby-Waite gave her delightfully rich laugh. "You are, of course, correct. Who on earth would stay in Cambridge?" Etta could almost hear the shudder in her voice.

They started chatting of other things, of a play they'd seen recently and whether it was an accurate representation of medieval France, completely unaware of the devastation they'd left in their wake.

Christopher would return to London.

Cold flashed through her. He would leave. Gwen would leave. They would both leave, and she would be left alone. Again.

Panic roared. Ducking her head, she pushed through the crowd. She saw nothing, heard nothing, only the sound of her heart too loud in her head, and her thoughts spiralled around her. Christopher *would* return to London, in a week's time he'd return, and she…she would remain here. And when he went back to London, when he had a society more intelligent than hers, more *learned* than hers, when he had beautiful women without carrot-red hair or overly passionate disposition, how long would it take him to forget her? Not at first. Oh no, he would be polite, and their correspondence would continue for a month, perhaps more. But then it would dwindle, then stop, and he'd forget. He'd forget about her, forget to send her articles, forget that once there was a girl he'd annoyed incessantly. He'd leave and he'd forget and she... She would be alone.

Somehow, she was in a room, an empty room. In the distance, laughter and music but here, here there was nothing but her thoughts.

Wrapping her arms about her stomach, she folded over at her waist. No one had ever wanted her, not enough to stay. She'd never known her mother, and her father was only ever interested in the law and his students. When he remembered he had a daughter, it was to tell her of her faults. In all her life there had only been Gwen, and Gwen, too, had left, first for London and the security of paid employment, and then for the duke. And now there was Christopher.

She dug her arms into her stomach, hard. Christopher, with his wicked smile and his way of annoying her until he drove her mad, only to kiss her anger away. Christopher, who understood her, who never disparaged her passion or her opinions, who stood by her side. He stood by her side, and that meant so much to her, it meant everything, and he was going to leave. He would return to London, and she would never— He would never—

Enough. By all that was holy, enough! She grabbed a hold of the emotion, the useless, stupid emotion, and took a breath, forcing her arms to her sides, forcing every muscle to relax, forcing her breath to calm. Christopher would leave. It was inevitable. He would return to London and she would be alone. She would not panic. She would not allow this useless emotion a voice. Everyone left.

It was inevitable.

***

CHRISTOPHER HELD ON TO his smile as yet another guest told him one of his novels was her very favourite and would he please give her a hint as to his next? In response, he gave a charming laugh and, with a wink, told her he couldn't give possibly divulge any hints. This was the reply he gave every guest who approached him, and as all before her, she tried again to glean some hint from him. He merely smiled mysteriously, all the while thinking of other places he'd rather be.

The afternoon tea soiree had teetered into early evening, and he'd tried to extricate himself numerous times. He'd been thwarted each time, another guest descending upon him to heap praise and ask questions that simply must be answered. The soiree was in support of the duchess's school and, as much as he thought it a worthy cause, four hours as the centre of attention was beginning to pall. Besides which, he hadn't had the glimpse of Etta for over an hour.

The duchess beamed at him from across the room, her delight at the success of the soiree palpable. Though most undoubtedly were here to see him, the attendance could only bode well for her school, and he could think of no more worthy cause for this inconvenient fame than to parlay it into goodwill for something long overdue.

From the corner of his eye, he saw a flash of carrot-red hair. A grin, natural and true, tugged at him. Finally.

Offering his excuses, he ignored any protest as he strode from the room, through the parlour doors, and into the garden. He was sure he'd seen her go past the rhododendron—

And there she was. Etta.

Something tight in him eased at the sight of her.

Hurrying to her side, he caught her in a bear hug, inhaling the fragrance of her carrot-red hair, lemons and sunshine.

She was stiff in his arms a moment before she relaxed, curving her body to his. Frowning, Christopher buried his nose in her hair. He was imagining things. She had never been rigid in his embrace before, but it was only because he hadn't seen her properly for two days, hadn't held her in his arms, felt her breath against his neck. She still smelled of violet and honeysuckle, and nothing had changed.

Belatedly, he realised she was pushing against his embrace. Frown deepening, he let her go. "Where did you disappear to?"

"What do you mean?" Taking a step from him, she curled her hair behind her ear.

"You weren't in the parlour." He'd never seen her fidget before. Unease crept along his spine.

"Gwen needed help elsewhere." Smoothing her hair behind her ear again, she lifted her chin.

Silence stretched between them. She folded her arms about herself, her hands gripping her biceps, forlorn and yet somehow defiant.

"What's the matter?" he finally said.

She didn't respond.

"Clearly, something is wrong." She wouldn't look at him, her head turned and eyes downcast. The skin of her cheek was smooth and pale. "Etta?"

Her hands tightened. "This has to end."

His own hands curled to fists, his nails digging into his flesh. "What does?"

"This. Us." Still she wouldn't look at him. "It has to end."

"Why?"

She laughed, the sound of it forced and broken. "You are to return to London next week. I am to continue with the school. We always knew this time would be finite."

"Did we. Did we know that." Muscle ticking in his jaw, he pressed his fists into his thighs.

Clearly unhappy with his answer, she tightened her hands further. "We can't continue."

"Why not?"

She averted her gaze. "Don't make this harder than it needs to be."

"Am I making it hard?" He smiled tightly. "I apologise."

She sighed impatiently.

"Don't do that. Don't you—" He took a breath, counted to five. "Why are you saying this, Etta? What's brought it on?"

"It's time." She lifted her chin. "We were never more than stolen moments, Christopher. You know that as well as I."

"Don't tell me what I know."

She ignored him. "No, it is simply better if we go on our separate ways. You'll give your speech tomorrow and then you'll return to London. You may continue to send articles to me, if you feel the need, but I shan't respond. I'll be busy, you understand, with the school. Gwen has asked me to teach, and though I intend to get my degree first, I have accepted. So, you see, there is no point to any of this. Good-bye, Lord Christopher." Without another word, she left, the ribbons on her gown trailing behind her.

Stock still, he stared at the empty space she had left. Abruptly, all anger drained from him. He couldn't think. Did she not know what she meant to him?

Swallowing, he forced himself to think logically. Why was she acting so? There was a reason, there had to be. If he could only think...He knew her. He knew her better than he knew himself and there had to be something, something that would make her break with him, leave him—

Of a sudden, it hit him. Leave him. Etta was leaving before she could be left.

He turned it over in his mind. It made sense. Everyone she'd cared for had left her in one way or another, and there had been no promises between them. He, like a fool, hadn't verbalised his thoughts, hadn't told her...

Bloody hell. He hadn't told her she was everything.

Calling himself every kind of fool, he made his way back into the ballroom. He needed a plan. He needed something to tell her what she meant to him, how he thought her magnificent.

He needed a gesture grand enough that even Henrietta Wilding-Marsh would believe.

Chapter Eleven

THE LECTURE HALL WAS fit to bursting. The chairs had filled over an hour ago, and though standing room was rapidly approaching capacity, people still spilled into the room, jostling each other to get a better vantage. Ladies who had the misfortune to stand fluttered their fans before them, more than one commenting loudly on the heat and stuffiness of the room while glaring at men who blatantly ignored them and continued to occupy seats. The raucous murmur of idle conversation filled the hall, the undercurrent heavy with anticipation. All were here to see Lord Christopher Hiddleston, and they were impatient for his arrival.

Etta paid no heed to the crowd surrounding her, her eyes locked on her clasped hands. Her gloves had yellowed with age, and one of the seams had started to unravel. Gwen had given her new gloves, fine kid leather in a rather shocking shade of red with seams so tight you could barely see the stitches. However, she couldn't bring herself to discard these, even though they'd already been old when she'd found them amongst those garments of her mother's her father hadn't discarded.

She started as Gwen bounced into the chair next to her, hugging a ledger to her chest, a happy smile wreathing her face. "This is simply unbelievable. Can you believe the hall is almost full?"

"Of course I can. I had no doubt."

Gwen's smile softened. "It's because of you, Etta. I couldn't have done this without you."

Etta plucked at the loose strand on her glove. "I haven't done much."

"You've done everything. I would never have had the notion or the confidence to do this without you." A frown flirted with Gwen's brow. "You know that, don't you?"

"I did little. You have done most of this."

"You were the one who led. All our lives, Etta. You showed me what could be, and not to accept what was. Don't you know how much you've influenced me?"

She ducked her head. "I got you into trouble more often than not."

"And I'm so grateful for that." Laying the ledger in her lap, Gwen took her hands. "You're my very best friend, and I would not have become the person I am today without you. I owe you everything." Grinning, Gwen squeezed her hands. "I love you dearly."

Eyes burning, a lump rose in her throat.

Gwen's brows drew together. "Etta?"

Wildly, she nodded, trying to work past the lump in her throat. She gasped and fought the burn in her eyes, but she lost. Tears spilled over. Wrenching her hands away, she swiped angrily at her cheeks.

Her friend looked alarmed. "Etta?"

"I'm fine. I'm fine, I promise." She smiled tremulously. "I love you, too."

Clearly unconvinced, Gwen laid her hand on her arm. "What is wrong?"

"Nothing, I—" She gave a watery sigh. That wouldn't fool Gwen. "I'll tell you after."

"Your Grace?" Miss Pelham, who they'd placed in charge of the event's schedule, hovered to the side. "I believe we're ready."

Gwen stood. "Yes, of course." Her gaze shifted to Etta. "You will tell me after."

"Yes."

Gwen looked at her a moment before nodding and allowing herself to be led away. Etta resumed contemplation of her gloves.

The murmurs around her grew more intense and then wild applause broke out. She tensed, her interlocked hands tightening.

He was here.

She couldn't resist. He stood to the left of Gwen, his gaze downcast as he waited. His hair was tousled, the auburn strands somehow glowing in the dull light of the hall, his suit jacket hugged his shoulders perfectly, and he wore a solemn expression, one she could not recall in all the years of knowing him.

Her heart ached, and she gripped her hands tight, forcing herself not to go to him. This would become less with time, this need, and it would dissipate entirely with his removal from Cambridge.

Gwen finished speaking. Etta had no idea what she'd said, but Christopher took the stage, his hands graceful as he arranged the notes on the lectern. She loved his hands, loved how they felt as they cradled her face, as he drew her in to his embrace. Stomach churning, she closed her eyes and willed herself to calm.

"Thank you all for coming today."

His voice washed over her, velvet and rich and a stroke along her skin. This would be the last time. After this, he would return to London and she would never hear his voice again, would never hear him say her name, hear the smile in his voice, hear the anticipation when he said something to deliberately rile her.

He wore a half-smile, a pale imitation of his usual brilliance. "I know you were hoping to hear an excerpt from my new novel, but instead I wrote something especially for today." Clearing his throat, he glanced down at the papers before him, his hands tightening on the lectern. "I wish to tell the tale of a girl who wanted impossible things."

He looked up, and his expression was more open, more vulnerable than she'd ever seen before. "From the time she was small, the girl wanted impossible things. She wanted to captain a pirate ship and fly to the moon. She wanted to dance and run and laugh, she wanted to be a queen and a fairy and a soldier and a hero, and she wanted to learn *everything*. Why the sky was blue, why two and three made five, why and how laws were made. More than anything, more than being a *pirate*, she wanted to learn."

Etta swallowed hard, her heart racing.

"The girl was often alone. Her mother had been stolen by an evil queen when the girl was but a babe, and her father had an evil enchantment, one that made the girl invisible to him. She learned to live with these things, to thrive in spite of them."

He was making a point. She was almost

certain...

"Others told her she couldn't have these things," he continued. "That she couldn't be a pirate, because she needed to behave. That she couldn't fly to the moon, because she had to be still. That she couldn't learn all the things in the world because it would make her peculiar and strange, and what girl would want to be peculiar and strange?

"The girl decided she didn't care for others' opinions, and so she set about to change the world."

Christopher's voice cracked. Clearing his throat, he regarded again the crowd. "She undertook a quest, and travelled for a year and a day, over stormy seas and deserts dry, until she found the place where impossible things lived. There, she could be a pirate, and she captained her ship with ferocity. She flew to moon, had tea and scones in a crater, and came back with tales of a dusty sea. She was a queen and a fairy and a soldier and a hero, and she learned everything she could."

His hands tightened on the lectern. "Having conquered these impossible things, she returned home, bringing them with her. But here's the thing about impossible things—they are ephemeral and easily lost. Somehow, along the way, she lost the proof of being a pirate and a queen, until all she brought home were the tattered memories of her achievements."

Gaze fixed, he cleared his throat again. "Of course, no one believed her. They thought her peculiar and strange, and though she protested, though she insisted, though she was serious and logical and passionate, no one took her seriously. No one believed her.

"Then, she met a boy who was never serious

about anything." Eyes trained on the papers before him, a slight smile lifted the corner of his lips. "This boy would argue with her, just to see her protest. He would laugh and prod, because he liked the fire in her eyes. He would do these things, but what he never told her, what he didn't want her to know, was that he believed. He believed she'd been a pirate queen, that she'd taken tea on the moon. He believed she'd learned all she could, that she was cleverer than him, and he knew that he admired her above all others on this earth. He also couldn't tell her that every time they'd argued, he'd given her a piece of his heart, until she owned all of it. But the boy, being foolish and never serious, could not tell her these things and the girl, being wise, strove to ignore him."

A lump rose again in her throat. He truly believed that?

"Years passed," he continued. "The boy pestered her from afar, knowing if she were annoyed, she would not forget him, even as he sought knowledge of her. He learned she had never forgotten her impossible things, that she strove daily to make them return.

"Then, one day, a truly miraculous thing was to occur. A great and fantastical structure was to be built, and the girl moved mountains and shifted rivers to make it happen. The boy, wanting her to have everything, did all he could to help. He, still foolish and still never serious, blundered. He did everything wrong, and the girl thought he didn't believe in her. That he would leave her. But the boy knew he never would. Never again. He would help her find the scattered and lost impossible things, would stand beside her as she fought to make others believe. He would do this for the rest of his life, if she would let him. And above all things, he would never leave her."

His gaze captured hers, refused to let her go. She swallowed, her heart wild in her chest.

He broke their gaze, swept the hall. "But that's just one more impossible thing, more fantastical than the rest." Here, he stopped.

Silence, a hush filled with expectation. Then, it erupted with wild applause.

Christopher bowed his head in thanks. The applause continued even after he'd gathered his papers, after he'd departed the lectern for the drawing room, after Gwen had taken his place, a bemused smile on her face as she waited for the applause to die down.

Etta took a shuddering breath. He had written something beautiful because he knew her. He knew her so well he'd created a fairy tale, and then he'd stood before all of Cambridge and spoken it.

She needed to speak with him. Rising, she headed for the drawing room.

***

HE STOOD BY THE window, looking out onto the street. His hands were braced on the sill, and his hair was tousled, as if he'd run his fingers through the dark auburn strands.

"Christopher," she said quietly, so quietly she didn't know if he'd heard her.

His shoulders tensed. He turned, his expression as solemn as ever she'd seen it. "Etta."

She didn't know what to do with her hands. "Your story was beautiful."

"Thank you."

"The girl... She was me?"

"Yes."

Silence stretched between them. He stood before her, so close, and all she could think was she'd tried to push him away. She'd told him to forget her, and instead he'd written that story, truth disguised as a fairy tale, and then he'd spoken it to all of Cambridge.

She didn't know what to say, completely at a loss how to articulate the swirl of her thoughts, the riot of her emotions. She didn't know, and he was looking at her, waiting for her to speak, and she couldn't. How was it she could argue on a hundred different things, debate a thousand topics, but now, when it was so important, she had not one word to say?

Silence grew, and she still didn't know what to say.

His eyes lost their light, becoming hard. "Was there something you wanted?" he asked flatly.

"I—" She swallowed, and tried again. "I—" She had to tell him. She had to tell him what his story meant to her, what he meant to her, but the words were frozen, stuck inside her, and no matter how she tried, she couldn't give them breath. "Christopher, I...I was...I shouldn't have..." Damnation, why couldn't she say what needed to be said?

Taking a step forward, and then another, he raised his hand to cup her cheek. "Etta," he said, and her name held longing and affection and exasperation and wryness and a hundred other things.

Shuddering, she closed her eyes and leaned into his touch, willing him to know, to feel what she wanted to say.

He traced her cheek with his thumb. "I've never left you, Etta. You've been first in my thoughts for so long, so that I don't know how to live if I don't have you in my head."

An involuntary noise of protest escaped. Opening her eyes, she found him gazing down at her, his dark eyes warm. So warm.

"I sent you those articles so you wouldn't forget me." The corner of his mouth lifted. "I knew as long as I annoyed you, you were thinking of me. I leapt at the chance to return to Cambridge, to help the duchess with her school, to help *you*. I thought, maybe, if I was fortunate and you didn't hate me, I could persuade you to spend time with me, even if only a moment. I wanted to spend time with you. I've *always* wanted to spend time with you." His thumb swept her skin. "I'm so damn glad it was more than a moment."

She leaned her forehead against his chest. He had the words, ones that held the ring of truth.

A broad hand made slow circles between her shoulder blades. "You told me to go, but how can I? I would be leaving you behind, and I can't do that, Etta. I want you with me. I want you scowling at me and telling me my characters are trite and my stories populous nonsense and forcing me to do better. I want to stand beside you when the school opens, to support you as you study, to applaud you when you get your law degree. All the days of my life, I want to share with you."

He was so vulnerable. How could he stand there and make himself so vulnerable?

"Etta, take as long as you need. I'm not going anywhere."

"That's just it," she burst out. "I want to believe. I want to trust that you'll stay, but I— Christopher, I—" Panic welled inside her. He would go, wouldn't he? Everyone always went.

"I won't ever leave you, Etta. Not willingly. Not ever." Gently, he pulled back. "Etta. My brave, bold, daring Etta. I love you." His gaze searched hers. "I love you."

She closed her eyes, swallowed. "You do?"

His lips whispered over her brow. "So much. And I will do this properly. I'll call on your father tomorrow, state my intentions."

"What intentions?" She couldn't think. Her brain wouldn't work, and she couldn't think.

Steady dark eyes held her gaze. "I'll never leave you."

Her mouth went dry. "You are the son of an earl."

"You are a gentleman's daughter. We are not so far apart."

Shaking her head, she pushed at his chest. "We are apart. We always will be. You are so far above me in consequence as to be laughable."

He refused to let her go. "Never, Henrietta Wilding-Marsh. I will never leave."

"Stop staying that." She shook her head. "You have to leave. You have commitments."

He shrugged. "Nothing that can't be amended."

"You have your writing."

"I can write here as much as I can in London."

"The business of an earldom."

"My brother is the earl, not I."

"You cannot change your life for me."

"You are not asking this of me, Etta. I am offering it."

Working her jaw, she searched his face. Calm, resolute, he met her gaze. "You won't leave?"

"Never."

Maybe…maybe he wouldn't. "I love you, too," she said, her voice small.

The corner of his mouth lifted. "I know."

"You know? How can you know? *I* didn't know."

He grinned. "You have a tell."

"A tell." Her jaw ticked.

His grin widened. "Yes."

"A tell. I have a tell. I'll have you know, sir, I have faced down many a man and they have never known what I was thinking."

"No, but those men didn't love you."

Instantly, her ire dissipated. "I have a tell?"

He nodded solemnly. "But only I know it."

She smiled, resting her head against his chest. She played with the button on his waistcoat. "You won't leave," she said, somehow certain.

"No." His arms tightened around her, and she felt warm and happy. She felt loved. "I won't."

Epilogue

Newspaper clipping sent to Miss Henrietta Wilding-Marsh, received 29 August 1849

This author cannot believe a Certain Lord who is also a Gothic Author of some renown has lingered so long in a University Town to the north. After his appearance at a Fundraising for a Scandalous College, his lordship has overstayed his visit, remaining in the university town for these three months and more, missing the Season and his brother's triumphant speeches in the House of Lords. His lordship, who himself has a Law Fellowship, shows no sign of returning to London.

This author wonders what is keeping him from our capital?

***

Newspaper clipping sent to Miss Henrietta Wilding-Marsh, received 15 October 1849

The Sowrith Law College for Women opened its

doors today, starting a truncated university year with a student body of twenty-three. This author is interested to see how long the school will be viable.

It should be noted famed Gothic author, Lord Christopher Hiddleston was in attendance. His lordship has become a fixture around Cambridge, and his speech to open the school was only superseded by Her Grace, the Duchess of Sowrith. Scandalously, the duchess is large with child and yet still showed herself in public.

***

Newspaper clipping sent to Miss Henrietta Wilding-Marsh, received 29 December 1849

...rumours abound at the D— of S— Christmas Ball held at B— C—. A certain lord who pens novels was seen to restrict his company only to a certain Miss W—-M—, which this author finds baffling. Miss W—-M— is known for her improper views and is herself studying at the Sowrith College for Women. How can it be his lordship finds her company desirable and, if the ring on her finger is any indication, looks to extend that company for a lifetime?

***

Newspaper clipping sent to Miss Henrietta Wilding-Marsh, received 15 May 1851

...the Gothic novelist has shifted genre with The Silence of Bells. A detective novel with the slightest of nods towards his Gothic roots, Lord Christopher has

created delightful characters in the persons of Edmund Ballantine and Lady Penelope. While this author is dispirited that we may have seen the last of his lordship's Gothics, it is with excitement that we embark on this new phase of Lord Christopher's career and if The Silence of Bells is any indication, it will be a long and fruitful one.

***

Newspaper clipping sent to Miss Henrietta Wilding Marsh, received 11 June 1853

Graduates: H. R. Wilding-Marsh, LL.B

***

Newspaper clipping sent to Miss Henrietta Wilding-Marsh, received 26 June 1853

29 June 1853 - I publish the banns of marriage between Lord Christopher Hiddleston of Tanworth-in-Arden, Warwickshire and Miss H. R Wilding-Marsh of Cambridge, Cambridgeshire.
This is the first time of asking. If any of you know cause or just impediment why these two persons should not be joined together in Holy Matrimony, ye are to declare it.

***

Newspaper clipping sent to Miss Henrietta Wilding-Marsh, received 3 July 1853

3 July 1853 - I publish the banns of marriage between Lord Christopher Hiddleston of Tanworth-in-Arden, Warwickshire and Miss H. R Wilding-Marsh of Cambridge, Cambridgeshire.

This is the second time of asking. If any of you know cause or just impediment why these two persons should not be joined together in Holy Matrimony, ye are to declare it.

***

Newspaper clipping sent to Miss Henrietta Wilding-Marsh, received 10 July 1853

10 July 1853- I publish the banns of marriage between Lord Christopher Hiddleston of Tanworth-in-Arden, Warwickshire and Miss H. R Wilding-Marsh of Cambridge, Cambridgeshire.

This is the third time of asking. If any of you know cause or just impediment why these two persons should not be joined together in Holy Matrimony, ye are to declare it.

***

Newspaper clipping sent to Lady Christopher Hiddleston (although she prefers H. R. Hiddleston), received 13 May, 1854

3 May - To Lord Christopher Hiddleston, LL.M and his wife, H.R Hiddleston, LL.B, a daughter.

***

My study, 13 May 1854

Dearest,
Thank you for sending me the newspaper notification of our daughter's birth. I might have missed it otherwise.

You know, you could send me an actual letter. I hear it is something people do.

Love,
Etta

***

Our drawing room, 13 May 1854

To my impossible girl, here is your letter.
I love you.
Christopher

Acknowledgments

Thank you to the judges of the Romance Writers of Austalia's Ruby Award. I gasped out loud when I saw Etta and Christopher's story had won, and I'm so stoked it was this novel in particular. This is my love letter to all those who try to effect change and who get constantly knocked back. It's hard to keep the fire burning and we all need someone to believe in us. Etta has Christopher, and Gwen, and the duke, and I hope you have someone as well.

Thank you, as always, to F4e, who *loved* Etta and Christopher and kept bugging me to 'hurry up and write their story'. Here 'tis, my friend.

Finally, thank you to everyone who helped along the way.

Read the first book in the Lost Lords series

FINDING LORD FARLISLE

The boy she never forgot

Lady Alexandra Torrence knows she's odd. Fascinated by spirits, she sets out to investigate rumours of a ghost at Waithe Hall, the haunt of her childhood. Its shuttered corridors stir her own ghosts: memories of the friend she'd lost. Maxim had been her childhood playmate, her kindred spirit, the boy she was beginning to love …but then he'd abandoned her, only to be lost at sea. She never expected to stumble upon a handsome and rough-hewn man who had made the Hall his home, a man she is shocked to discover is Maxim: alive, older…and with no memory of her.

The girl he finally remembers

Eleven years ago, a shipwreck robbed Lord Maxim Farlisle of his memory. Finally remembering himself, he journeys to his childhood home to find Waithe Hall shut and deserted. Unwilling to face what remains of his family, Maxim makes his home in the abandoned hall only to have a determined beauty invade his uneasy peace. This woman insists he remember her and slowly, he does. Once, he and Alexandra had been inseparable, beloved friends who were growing into something more…but the reasons he left still exist, and how can he offer her a broken man?

As the two rediscover their connection, the promise of young love burns into an overwhelming passion. But the time apart has scarred them both—will they discover a love that binds them together, or will the past tear them apart forever?

Read an Excerpt from
FINDING LORD FARLISLE
Lost Lords, Book One

Chapter One

Northumberland, England, August 1819

LIGHTNING STREAKED ACROSS THE darkening sky and thunder followed. Stillness held sway a moment, the air thick, before a torrent of rain battered the earth.

Wrestling against the wind, Lady Alexandra Torrence tucked her portmanteau closer to her person as she pushed determinedly toward the estate looming in the distance. The storm had been but a sun-shower when she'd set out from Bentley Close, her family's estate only a half hour walk. While the light cloak she wore protected her from the worst of it, the wet was beginning to seep into her skin.

She pulled her cloak tighter. It was only a little farther and she'd be at Waithe Hall, though there would be no one to greet her. Waithe Hall had been closed for years, ever since the previous earl had died. The new earl—Viscount Hudson, as he'd once been—resided almost exclusively in London. Her family and his had been close for as long as she could remember, their townhouses bordering each other in London just as their estates did here in Northumberland. The earl was her elder by nine years, and his brother Stephen by five, but Maxim, the youngest, had been but one year her senior and—

She stopped that thought in its tracks.

Before too much longer she stood before the entrance to Waithe Hall, and with it, shelter. The huge wooden doors were shut. She could not recall that she had ever seen them closed and locked. In the past when she'd visited the family had been in residence so she would walk straight in, calling for Maxim before she'd completely cleared the entrance—

Slowly, she exhaled. After a moment, she pulled the key from her pocket, the one Maxim had given to her for safekeeping when he was ten and she nine, so they could always find their way back in should the doors ever be locked—

Shoving the key into the lock, she blinked fiercely as she forced memory aside once more. She could do this. It had been years, the wound so old it should have long since faded. She could investigate Waithe Hall and its ghosts, and she would not think of him.

The key turned easily, the door swinging open. She stepped inside. Cavernous silence greeted her, the din of the rain that had been so deafening now distant. The entrance stretched before her, disappearing into darkness, and the storm had made the late afternoon darker than usual, swallowing any light that peeked through closed doors. Pausing mid-step, she wondered if perhaps she had made a mistake in coming here.

Shaking off doubt, she started through the hall. The rain echoed through the vastness, the hollow sound strange after being caught in its fury. Fumbling through her portmanteau she found a candle and tinder.

The flickering light revealed an entrance corridor that opened into an enclosed court encompassing the first and second floors and an impressive chandelier draped in protective cloth hung at its centre. Memory painted it with crystal and candles, and she remembered sitting on the landing of the second floor, legs dangling through the gaps between balusters as she and Maxim counted the crystals for the hundredth time.

Bowing her head, she cursed herself. She should have known she could not keep the memories at bay.

A roll of thunder reverberated around her, leaving behind quiet and dark. All her memories of Waithe Hall were full of life, the butler directing servants, fresh flowers in the vases lining the court, light spilling through from the mammoth windows. Now the windows were shuttered, and an eerie silence broken only by the sounds of the storm pervaded.

Hitching her bag, she made her way to the sitting room. It was as still as the rest of the estate, the furniture draped in holland covers, the windows also shuttered. Setting her candle down, she placed her cloak over the back of a chair and rested her bag on its seat, glancing nervously about. She caught herself. *Don't be stupid, Alexandra. There's none here.*

Before she could think further, she unbuttoned

her bodice. Her clothes were soaked, uncomfortably damp against her skin, and a chill was beginning to seep through, though it was the tail end of summer and the days were still mostly warm. She'd chosen a simple gown, one she knew she could get into and out of herself.

Heat rose on her cheeks as she shucked out of the bodice. There was none here. She knew there was no one. Cheeks now burning, she untied her skirt and petticoats, left only in her stays and chemise. She would love to remove her stays as well, but they were only slightly damp and she couldn't bring herself to disrobe more than she had.

Opening her bag, she pulled out a spare bodice, skirt, petticoats and, finally, a towel. Thanking her stars she'd had the forethought to bring it, she quickly swiped herself, chanting all the while there was no one watching her, that doing this in an abandoned sitting room was not immodest.

In record time, she'd managed to reclothe herself. Hanging her wet clothes to dry, she pushed her hair out of her face. Once she had explored further, she would choose one of the bedchambers as her base, but for right now the sitting room would suffice.

A thread of guilt wound through her. Technically, the earl did not know she was a guest of Waithe Hall—and by technically, she meant he didn't know at all. She was confident however, he could have no objection. She had been a regular presence at Waithe Hall when she was a girl, and the earl held some affection for her. She was almost positive. Maxim had often said his brother thought her—

Damnation. Bracing herself against a chair, she bowed her head. She had thought more of him in the last hour than she had in the year previous. It was this place. She'd managed to convince herself she no longer felt the sharp bite of grief, but she did. It struck her at odd moments, and she could never predict when. One would think it would have lessened with time, but it hit her fresh and raw, as if she bled all over again. She'd been a fool to think she would remain unaffected returning here—he was everywhere.

She closed her eyes as realisation cut through her. She was going to think of him. It was inevitable. However, she had come here with purpose and she would not allow this preoccupation to deter her.

The ghosts of Waithe Hall beckoned.

A darkening gloom shrouded the drawing room. Night approached, quicker than she'd liked, but she was determined to at least do a preliminary sweep of the estate to refresh her memory before it became too dark to continue. There was much to do before she camped out in the affected room one night soon, not the least of which was determining which room was affected.

From her bag, she pulled a compass, a ball of twine, and her notebook. Bending over the flickering light of her candle, she opened her notebook and dated the page, jotting down her notes on the expedition thus far.

There had always been tales of ghosts at Waithe Hall. On her and Maxim's frequent rides about the estate, she remembered listening wide-eyed as Timmons had told them tales of ghosts and woe. The groom had waxed lyrical on the myths and legends of spiritual activity at Waithe Hall, and she'd been completely fascinated. Maxim had never seemed interested, but he'd always followed when she'd concocted a new adventure to discover ghosts and ghouls. As an adult, she'd turned her fascination into a hobby, researching and cataloguing ghost tales at every manor and estate she'd attended. Her own family's estate held a ghost or two, stories her father had been only too happy to tell. She'd documented his tale and others, and had submitted several articles to the Society for the Research of Psychical Phenomena. They hadn't as yet chosen to publish any of them, but she was convinced if she persisted, eventually they would.

Then, four months ago, reports had crossed the earl's desk in London of strange lights at Waithe Hall. He'd mentioned it in passing to her father, who in turn, knowing her fascination, had mentioned it to her. He'd also issued a stern warning she was not to pursue an investigation but, well, she was twenty-five years old and in possession of an inheritance a great aunt had left her. Her father could suggest, but he could not compel.

The lights could be any number of things, but the report had contained accounts of a weeping woman, and the light had become a search light. Memory reminded her of a tale Timmons had told, the lament of a housekeeper of Waithe Hall who had lost a set of keys and caused a massacre. Her lips quirked. Timmons' tales had ever been grisly.

Determination had firmed and within a week she'd made her way to Northumberland and Waithe Hall. Bentley Close had been shut as well, but unlike Waithe Hall, a skeleton staff kept the estate running. Along with her maid, Alexandra had arrived late last night though she hadn't been in a position to set out for Waithe Hall until late this afternoon. Her plan had always been to spend a few days here, but the rain made it so she now had no choice.

She would rather be here than in London anyway. Besides pretending she was unaffected by those who called her odd, her younger sister had finally made her debut at the grand old age of twenty. Lydia was taking society by storm, determined to wring every ounce of pleasure out of her season, and she had confidently informed their parents she didn't intend to wed until she had at least three seasons behind her. At first horrified, their parents had resigned themselves to neither of their daughters marrying any time soon.

As the eldest of her parents' children and a female besides, she had borne the brunt of their expectations in that respect, but at least Harry had now brought them some joy. He and Madeline Pike were to marry next year, the wedding of the heir to a marquisette and a duke's daughter already touted as the event of the season. George had absconded to the continent, no doubt investigating the most macabre medical reports he could, while Michael was still at Eton.

Upstairs, a door slammed shut. Alexandra jumped, hand flying to her racing heart. It was the wind. It had to be. Even now it howled outside, rain pelting the roof and echoing through the hall as distant thunder rolled.

Hugging the notebook to her chest, she shucked off any concerns. There was no time like the present. She would start with an examination of the ground floor. The kitchens and servants rooms would take an age, so better to examine the family rooms and save the servants for another time.

The portrait gallery was as she remembered, a long stretch of hall that displayed the Farlisles in all their permutations. Quickly, she traversed its length, telling herself the dozens of eyes of previous Farlisles did not follow her, that they did not judge her an unwelcome guest. Cold slid up her spine and she moved faster, especially as she passed the portrait of the old earl and his sons, Maxim staring solemnly from the portrait.

Pretending she felt not a skerrick of unease, she noted the gallery's dimensions in her diary and moved on to the second sitting room. Again, nothing in particular was out of the ordinary.

The library was at the end of the corridor, and the door opened easily under her hand. It really was most obliging of the steward not to have locked any of the doors inside the estate. This room was vastly different to her remembrance. Few books lined the shelves thick with dust, and holland covers draped most of the furniture, although one of the high-backed arm chairs before the fire was lacking the covering. Peculiarly, one of the windows here was unshuttered, the weak light of storm-dampened twilight casting eerie shadows on the wall opposite.

She'd always loved the library and its two storeys containing rows upon rows of books. As children, she'd insisted she and Maxim spend an inordinate amount of time within its walls, happily miring herself in book after book. Maxim had always been bored within seconds, spending his time tossing his ever-present cricket ball higher and higher in the air to see if he could hit the ceiling two floors above. He'd even managed it, a time or two.

Sharp pain lodged beneath her breast. Rubbing at her chest, she took a breath against it, pulling herself to the present. Somehow, night had encroached upon the room. How long had she been stood there, lost in memory?

Moving further into the room, she trailed her fingers over the side table next to the undraped chair. A stack of thick books was piled high, the top one containing a marker. Why was there a stack of books? Had an apparition placed them there?

A prickle rippled along her skin. She'd never seen a ghost. She'd heard hundreds, thousands of stories, but she'd never— Steadying herself, she flipped open the book to the spot marked, noting it was a history of the Roman invasion and settlement of Cumbria. Sections and rows were underlined with pencil, writing filled the margins, and there was something about the hand….

Closing the book, she placed it back on the stack. Why was this here? Every other part of Waithe Hall she'd seen had been closed, shut away. This room held an uncovered chair, a stack of books and…. The fireplace held recent ashes.

Her heart began to pound.

Again, something—a door?—banged. Whirling around, she searched the encroaching dark, her gaze desperate as her chest heaved. What if the lights weren't a ghost? What if it was a vagrant, someone dangerous and unkind? What if…what if it were a *murderer*?

The agitated sound of her breathing filled the room. Getting a hold of herself, she reined in her imaginations. Her thoughts could—and frequently did—run to the extreme. Although these anomalies were curious, there could be a perfectly mundane reason for their presence. There was nothing out of the ordinary, besides the books, and the fireplace, and—

She took a breath. *Calm, Alexandra.* She was

purportedly an investigator. She would investigate.

The fireplace had without doubt been used recently. Newly cut logs placed in a neat pile to the side. Sconces held half-used candles, their wicks blackened and bodies streaked with melted wax. She could see no other signs of occupation—

Something banged for a third time, closer now, and brought with it a howling wind. Alexandra jumped, grabbing at the table for balance as the door to the library flew open, the heavy wood banging against the wall, the books wobbling and threatening to fall. Blood pounding in her ears, she looked to the darkened maw of the library's entrance.

An indistinct white shape filled the door, hovering at least five feet above the floor.

A scream lodged in her throat. She couldn't move, couldn't make a sound. She could only stare as the thing approached.

Lightning crashed, flashing through the room. She gasped, a short staccato sound that did little to unlock her chest.

Lightning crashed again. The shape became distinct in the brief flash of light, revealing a man dressed in shirt sleeves and breeches, his dark hair long about his harsh face. A strong, handsome face that held traces of the boy she'd thought never to see again.

Blood drained from her own face, such she felt faint. "Maxim?"

Chapter Two

"WHAT ARE YOU DOING here?" it—he—
growled.

"Maxim?" she repeated stupidly. The apparition
before her looked so much like Maxim...if Maxim
had grown to a man, developed an abundance of
muscle and four inches of height. It couldn't be
Maxim...but if it were an apparition, why would he
appear grown? When last she'd seen him, he'd been
fifteen and skinny as a reed, not much taller than she.
It couldn't be him.

Lightning lit the room once more. His shirt was
loose about his thighs, the ties undone and the neck
gaping open, his breeches smudged with dirt. All was
well tailored and untattered. Surely, if he were a
ghost, his raiments should be tattered?

The same chestnut hair fell over his brow, too
long and ragged, while his face had broadened and
hardened, his eyes were the same, chocolate brown
under dark brows. He'd grown to a man, broad
shoulders and ropy muscle apparent behind the scant
clothes he wore, his breeches stretched over powerful

thighs and strong calves, his large feet shod in well-worn leather boots.

He was supposed to be dead. Eleven years ago, he had abruptly left Eton and set sail on one of the Roxwaithe ships, bound for America. She'd been so confused at the time, and he'd refused to tell her why. Six months later, they had received word the ship had been lost at sea. None had survived.

With startling clarity, she remembered that day. Her father's face, careworn and concerned, as he'd told her. Her mother's worried eyes. The pain in her chest, frozen at first, until she'd excused herself, blindly making her way to her chamber only to stand in its centre, confusion filling her until she'd happened to glance upon his cricket ball, the one he'd given her the last time she'd seen him, three days before he'd left when he'd refused to tell her why he was leaving, and once she'd returned home she'd thrown it onto her dressing table, angry beyond belief at him, that he was going away, and then, then a great gaping hole had cracked open inside her and she'd slid to the floor, pain and grief and devastation growing inside her until it had encompassed all, it had encompassed everything and it hadn't stopped, it hadn't stopped, it—

It was eleven years ago. The pain had faded, but had never truly left. She'd thought she'd learned to live with it. But now…he was here?

A thunderous scowl on his face, he made a noise of impatience. "I do not have the inclination for this, girl. Tell me why you have come."

His voice crashed over her. That, too, had deepened with age, but it was him. It was *him*.

"It *is* you." Joy filled her, so big it felt her skin couldn't contain it. Throwing herself at him, she enveloped him in a hug.

He stiffened.

Embarrassment coursed through her. What was she thinking? Immediately, she untangled herself from him. "I beg your pardon," she stammered. Always before they'd been exuberant in their affections. They'd always found ways to touch one another, even though that last summer, the one before he'd gone away, she'd begun to feel...more.

Clasping her hands before her, she brought herself to the present. Much had changed, now they were grown and he, apparently, had not died.

Maxim had not died.

A wave of emotion swept her, a mix of relief, joy, incredulity.... It buckled her knees and burned her eyes. He was alive. *Maxim was alive.*

"When did you return? Do your brothers know?" she asked, steadying herself as she swiped at the wetness on her cheeks. "The earl is lately in London, but I'm certain he would return should he know. My father will be so pleased to see, as will my mother. George and Harry will be beside themselves, and Lydia and Michael too, though they were so young when—" She cut herself off, barely able to say the word *died.* "We mourned you, Maxim."

He came closer. He'd grown so tall. When last she'd seen him, barely an inch had separated them, but now he was at least two hands taller. Faint lines fanned from his eyes, the tanned skin shocking in the cold English weather. Wherever he'd been, it had been sunburned.

"I ask again," he said. "Why have you come?"

Confusion drew her brows. "Maxim? Don't you remember me?"

Starting at the blonde hair piled limply on her

head thanks to the rain, he ran his gaze over her. He traced her face, her throat, travelled over her chest, swept her legs. A tingling began within her, gathering low. She was suddenly aware of how her breasts pushed against the fabric of her chemise with every breath, of a pulse between her legs that beat slow, steady....

He raised his gaze to hers. Silence filled the space between them before, succinctly, "No."

It was like a punch to her belly. "It's me. Alexandra."

No reaction.

Oh. Oh, this hurt.

Lifting her chin, she managed, "I am Lady Alexandra Torrence, daughter of your neighbour, the Marquis of Strand. We grew up together."

His expression did not change.

"Your father, the previous earl, and mine were like brothers."

He stared at her. "Previous earl?" he finally asked.

"Yes," she said. "Your father passed away some years ago. Your eldest brother is now earl."

Again, no change in expression. Did he not care his father had died? But what did she know of this new Maxim? Less than an hour ago, she had not known he was alive.

He continued to stare at her. She fought the urge to shift under that flat gaze. "Why are you here?" he repeated, his tone harsh and impatient.

"I was—" Her voice cracked. Cursing her nerves, she cleared her throat. "I am investigating. The villagers spoke of a ghostly presence, lights and wails, and I...." She trailed off. Lord, it made her sound so odd. He'd always teased her about that oddness, and always with affection. She didn't know what this new Maxim would do.

Finally there was expression on his face. She wished it had remained stony. "Ghosts? You have invaded my home for ghosts?"

The disgust in his voice made her cringe. "To be fair, I didn't know you were here. No one did."

Expression still disdainful, he didn't reply.

Irritation pushed aside devastation. How could he not remember *her*? "This is not *your* home."

His brows shot up. "*That* is your argument?"

He sounded so much like *her* Maxim. They'd argued often, and the number of times he'd said those exact words, in that exact tone…. She shook herself. "Yes. It is."

"A fallacy. You argue a fallacy."

"It is not a fallacy. It is objectively true. Waithe Hall is the ancestral seat of the Earls of Roxwaithe. You are not the Earl of Roxwaithe, ergo, it is not your home." Knowing it was childish, she tossed her hair and glared.

Crossing his arms, he scowled. "I know you are somewhere you don't belong."

"So are you," she pointed out.

"This is my family home."

"It's your *brother's*," she said. "You're being deliberately obtuse."

"And you're being obstinate."

"*I'm* being obstinate? Me?" This was such a ridiculous argument, and yet it was familiar. They'd argued like this all the time, and he was reacting exactly as her Maxim would react, and—

Stepping forward, he deliberately loomed over her. "I come into my library to find a trespasser, poking around in *my* things."

"Waithe Hall is shut. Roxwaithe hasn't been here in years. *No one* is supposed to be here. You aren't even supposed to be *alive*. How are you even *feeding* yourself?"

Pinching the bridge of his nose, he shook his head. "Why am I arguing with you? You're a trespasser I don't know."

Rage, such as she'd never experienced before, exploded. How dare he? How dare he pretend not to know her? Her fingers curled into fists and she told herself she could not punch him. She was a lady, and he was a *clodpole*. "Don't be *stupid*."

He stilled, and something flickered in his dark eyes. "You will leave the way you came."

"With pleasure," she snapped. Pushing past him, she stalked from the library, through the entrance hall, and wrenched the door open. Rain pelted her, almost horizontal as the wind howled and lightning crashed across the sky. She plunged into it, anger propelling her even as she was drenched in moments.

She'd not gotten more than two strides before a large hand grabbed her shoulder and hauled her back inside. Maxim slammed the door shut and shook himself, water falling to the marble floor. "Do you have any brains?" he demanded.

"You told me to go. I have no desire to say here with *you*."

"You wouldn't get half a mile before you'd catch your death. You'll stay here."

"It would not be proper," she said stiffly.

He laughed harshly. "Hunting a ghost is not proper, either. You will stay here."

Mutinously, she glared at him. Damnation. She could not even *argue* that point. Belatedly, she realised the rain had plastered his shirt to his body, clinging to hard muscle and broad shoulders.

Mouth abruptly dry, her breath locked in her chest.

He didn't seem to notice her distraction. "Come," he said, holding aloft a lamp he'd magically produced, before turning on his heel to stride down the corridor. Hesitantly, she followed.

They wound through the Hall, climbing the grand stairs and making their way to the family apartments, the corridors she remembered from her—their—childhood. Wrapping her arms about herself, she cursed herself at the soaked fabric. She'd only brought two gowns, and now both were wet.

He halted before a door. "You may stay here," he said, pushing it open.

Passing him, she entered a bedchamber, again with most of the furniture covered. The bed, though, was not, holding a mattress along with pillows and sheets.

Surprise filled her. "Is this where you sleep?"

He placed the lamp on the dresser. "Goodnight."

"Good—?" He was gone before she finished the word.

Wrapping her arms about her torso, she stopped herself from rushing after him. She wanted to assure herself she hadn't imagined him, that he was real, that he was alive…and she needed to get her bag, she had a nightgown and a change of underclothes, and—Maxim was alive.

She collapsed onto the bed. The bed he had slept in, unmade with the sheets rucked to the foot of the bed. A faint scent wound about her, woodsy and indistinct, but she knew it was his, knew it was

Maxim's. A harsh sob broke from her, and another, eleven years of emotion exploding. Sliding from the bed, she pulled herself into a ball, hot forehead against her updrawn knees, her cheeks wet, her chest hurting.

The wind howled, rain pelting the window. They'd all thought him dead. *She'd* thought him dead. Her dearest companion, her best friend. Maxim.

Slowly, her sobs subsided. She couldn't stay here. She couldn't take his bed from him, and she.... She wanted to know. She wanted to know everything. Why was he here? Why hadn't he gone to his brothers? Why was he lurking in Waithe Hall alone? When had he returned?

Did he really not remember her?

Taking a shuddering breath, she wiped at her cheeks. She needed to know and surely he would tell her. Even if he didn't remember her.

Rising to her feet, she squared her shoulders. Well, she would make him remember her...and then she would make him let her hug him.

TEACH ME

by Cassandra Dean

Ever curious, Elizabeth, Viscountess Rocksley, has turned her curiosity to erotic pleasure. Three years a widow, she boldly employs the madam of a brothel for guidance but never had she expected her education to be conducted by a coldly handsome peer of the realm.

To the Earl of Malvern, the erotic tutelage of a skittish widow is little more than sport, however the woman he teaches is far from the mouse he expects. With her sly humor and insistent joy, Elizabeth obliterates all his expectations and he, unwillingly fascinated, can't prevent his fall.

Each more intrigued than they are willing to admit, Elizabeth and Malvern embark upon a tutelage that will challenge them, change them, come to mean everything to them...until a heartbreaking betrayal threatens to tear them apart forever.

SILK & SCANDAL
THE SILK SERIES, BOOK 1

by Cassandra Dean

Eight years ago...
Thomas Cartwright and Lady Nicola Fitzgibbons
were friends. Over the wall separating their homes,
Thomas and Nicola talked of all things – his studies
to become a barrister, her frustrations with a lady's
limitations.

All things end.
When her diplomat father gains a post in Hong Kong,
Nicola must follow. Bored and alone, she falls into
scandal. Mired in his studies of the law and aware of
the need for circumspection, Thomas feels forced to
sever their ties.

But now Lady Nicola is back…and she won't let him
ignore her.

ROUGH DIAMOND
THE DIAMOND SERIES, BOOK 1

by Cassandra Dean

Owner of the Diamond Saloon and Theater, Alice Reynolds is astounded when a fancy Englishman offers to buy her saloon. She won't be selling her saloon to anyone, let alone a man with a pretty, empty-headed grin…but then, she reckons that grin just might be a lie, and a man of intelligence and cunning resides beneath.

Rupert Llewellyn has another purpose for offering to buy the pretty widow's saloon—the coal buried deep in land she owns. However, he never banked on her knowing eyes making him weak at the knees, or how his deception would burn upon his soul.

Each determined to outwit the other, they tantalize and tease until passion explodes. But can their desire bridge the lies told and trust broken?

About Cassandra Dean

Cassandra Dean is an award-winning author of historical and fantasy romance. She grew up daydreaming, inventing fantastical worlds and marvellous adventures. Once she learned to read (First phrase – To the Beach. True story), she was never without a book, reading of other people's fantastical worlds and marvellous adventures.

Cassandra is proud to call South Australia her home, where she regularly cheers on her AFL football team and creates her next tale.

Connect with Cassandra

cassandradean.com

facebook.com/AuthorCassandraDean

twitter.com/authorCassDean

instagram.com/authorcassdean

bookbub.com/authors/cassandra-dean

To learn about exclusive content, upcoming releases
and giveaways,
join Cassandra's mailing list:

cassandradean.com/extras/subscribe

Printed in Great Britain
by Amazon

82541900R00099